THE HOUSE OF PAIN,
or,
THE GIANT RAT OF SUMATRA

By Stephen Seitz

Paperback ISBN 978-1-78092-761-9
ePub ISBN 978-1-78092-762-6
PDF ISBN 978-1-78092-763-3

Published in the UK by MX Publishing
335 Princess Park Manor, Royal Drive,
London, N11 3GX www.mxpublishing.co.uk
Cover design by www.staunch.com

INTRODUCTION

"The only island known to exist in the region in which my uncle was picked up is Noble's Isle, a small volcanic islet and uninhabited. It was visited in 1891 by H. M. S. Scorpion. A party of sailors then landed, but found nothing living thereon except certain curious white moths, some hogs and rabbits, and some rather peculiar rats." – Charles Edward Prendick, *The Island of Dr. Moreau*

At long last, I can give the world the truth behind Sherlock Holmes' reference to the Giant Rat of Sumatra, and how events brought Holmes together with the infamous Dr. Alexandre Moreau, and with one of the 19th century's most noted zoologists, one George Edward Challenger, long before the latter's adventures recounted in *The Lost World*.

Before I begin, those readers unfamiliar with *The Island of Dr. Moreau* should probably skip this introduction to avoid spoilers. As for Challenger, I reveal nothing not already known to millions of readers everywhere.

For decades, students of the life of Sherlock Holmes have wondered about The Giant Rat of Sumatra, first mentioned in Dr. John Watson's account of the Sussex Vampire, published in 1924. At the time, Sherlock Holmes did not deem the world ready to accept the existence of such a creature, and we now know, thanks to the book you hold in your hands, that Holmes wanted to suppress a good deal more than that.

Those who have read *Sherlock Holmes and the Plague of Dracula* know how I came to possess Dr. John Watson's journals, during which he recorded the events of his daily life; those, of course, include his time with Sherlock Holmes. The journals do a lot to straighten out Watson's incoherent sense of dating. As I mentioned in *SHPoD*, Watson could not publish fully accurate accounts of Holmes' adventures due to the risk of libel, not to mention the risk of angering the British government. One suspects that Watson was protected by Mycroft Holmes without his knowledge at Sherlock's request. It is widely known, and admitted by Watson in some stories, that he had to alter names, dates, and other identifying data, if only to avoid scandal for innocent parties. I also believe that Watson followed the old adage, "Never let the facts get in the way of a good story."

The miracle of this particular manuscript, which I am calling *The House of Pain*, is that the dating adds up between Edward Prendick's account of *The Island of Dr. Moreau* and the dates given by Watson in "The Reigate Squires." Sherlockian chronologists agree, for once, that the latter case took place in April 1887. While Prendick was not able to precisely mark his time on the island, he does give us one telling clue: Dr. Moreau dies on the full moon. Using Prendick's rough chronology, that means it could only have happened on March 8, 1887, well within the dates given by Watson for "The Reigate Squires."

For those not familiar, that story opens with Watson heading to the French city of Lyon, where Holmes has been laid low with exhaustion, the result of an intense two-month investigation for the Netherland Sumatra company and its being swindled out of millions by Baron Maupertius, the Bernard Madoff of his day.

"Even his iron constitution," Watson tells us, "had broken down under the strain of an investigation which had extended over two months, during which period he had never worked less than fifteen hours a day, and had more than once, as he assured me, kept to his task for five days at a stretch."

"Aha!" I hear some of you saying. "Holmes could

not have been both tracking Alexandre Moreau and Baron Maupertius at the same time!"

Well, guess what? He could. Though Watson's stories tell one tale at a time, every journalist and private investigator can tell you it doesn't work that way. Of course Holmes worked on more than one case at the same time. The rent doesn't get paid any other way. If you work for yourself, you take as much work as you can handle, and sometimes you take on too much. Keeping up with it all can easily take up to 15 hours a day, and that's no doubt what Holmes did. In early 1887, Holmes was chasing down the giant rats, trying to locate and stop Dr. Moreau, and at the same time accommodate the Netherland Sumatra Company's troubles. As it happened, that particular affair turned out to be a disaster for the Moreau family, which had heavy investments in Sumatra. None of that, however, has anything to do with the narrative I present here. If it doesn't advance the story, it doesn't go in. Interested researchers will just have to do their own legwork.

As I did with *SHPoD*, I had to go to other archives to find supplementary information and to confirm the facts. The descendants of the Moreau family, I am sorry to say, threw up every roadblock they could; Alexandre's infamy endures to this day, and they want nothing to do with him. Luckily, there is enough information extant in public records so that, in the end, I did not need their help. The family's cooperation, however, would have provided a fuller narrative. For one thing, I never did determine what happened to Moreau's niece, Sophie, on her sojourn to America.

The Challenger papers proved somewhat less daunting, but still required me to spend a lot of time and effort. The man was an inconsistent diarist, although his researches were always precise. The tough part, it turned out, was finding his journals. All of Challenger's academic work has been either posted online, or is readily available from specialized libraries.

The journals, and their gold mine of personal information, seemed to have disappeared. No one in the Challenger family today had ever seen them, the universities where Challenger spent his days did not have them, but once I tracked down the law firm Challenger used for his personal affairs, I found the records of an estate sale in their dusty files. (Challenger lived well into the mid-20th century.) The Challenger journals had gone to a manuscript dealer in London, who had sold them to a private collector of dinosaur memorabilia, who asked me not to reveal his identity. You'll just have to take my word for their authenticity.

Moreau scholars, I'm afraid, will find this narrative of little help in trying to find the actual island. Both the logs of the *Meribelle* and the *Mississippi Delta* are silent on the subject, no doubt due to pressure from the Moreau family. C.E. Prendick records that some of the Moreau rats made it as far as Noble's Isle, but that tells us nothing; the sailors would have found the ruins of the Moreau compound and the House of Pain had they been on Noble's Isle.

One last note: I have changed the spelling and punctuation from the original British to American usage. My damned computer won't obey me and autocorrects every other word. I have just plain given up.

We now live in a world where gene splicing is routine, cloning commonplace, and the art of anesthesia is far advanced from the time of Dr. Moreau. Despite Holmes' admonition, I think the world can handle the cruel misdeeds of one deranged scientist. I thank readers for their indulgence.

Stephen Seitz
Springfield, Vt.

4

From the Journals of Dr. John H. Watson, M.D.

January 21, 1887

The horrible tragedy in Spitalfields earlier this week has had some unexpected bonuses, not the least of which is ending a long period of boredom for my friend Sherlock Holmes. Now he can put that blasted needle away.

The cocaine may relieve his ennui between clients, but it is no honeymoon in Paris for those of us who have to endure it. His moods range from manic to melancholy; he'll index documents for hours on end, or stare out the window for so long at a time one might think he had died in his armchair.

On Wednesday last, some seventeen people were crushed to death in the panic following a false fire alarm at the Hebrew Dramatic Club, in Princes' Street. The press accounts claim that not long after, what might have been an unremarkable incident turned to terror because someone thought a gas leak to blame, and as a consequence cut off the supply. This action plunged the building into complete darkness, and the only way in or out is through a private residence which has been converted into a club.

The play that night was in Hebrew, Spitalfields being where London's foreign Jews seem to congregate. The proceeds were intended to benefit an ailing Jewish workman, but now money is needed for funeral costs. When I heard the reluctant trudge of a client up our well-worn steps, I had no idea that Holmes and I would be drawn into the disaster's sequel.

Three sad, reluctant knocks brought me to the door. To my surprise, the nervous, dejected man I admitted into our rooms had a familiar face, and it took me a moment to realize we had played rugby together in my army days, to pass the time between battles.

"Hastings!" I cried. "Can it be you?"

He gazed at me for a moment, smiled with recognition, and said, "Upon my soul, it isn't John Watson, is it? You played forward. They couldn't get a ball past you, could they?"

Hastings had changed little over the past 15 years or thereabouts. His tie and tweeds marked him as an upper middle class Englishman, and he carried a black walking stick capped with a brass knob. In height a head shorter than myself, but he would still be able to wear the old uniform, which I am humbled to admit I no longer can.

"I haven't heard from you in ages," I said. "What brings you here?"

"A deeply distressing personal problem," said Holmes, rising, still in the mouse grey dressing gown he had donned that morning. "That much is evident from your expression. You are a cabinetmaker and purveyor of home furnishings, I perceive."

"How could you know that?" our guest asked.

"You are dressed too well for work in a standard woodshop, and you are dressed like a businessman. Quite successful, too, to judge from your new walking stick. Combine that with the lingering aroma of varnish, I conclude not only that you sell home furnishings, but make some of them yourself."

"I see you have warranted your reputation, Mr. Holmes. Yes, you are quite right. I made my beginning as a cabinetmaker, but I now have my own establishment. I find the work relaxing and rewarding, and there is a certain pride in knowing I can compete with the best of them."

"I must make introductions," I said. "Mr. Sherlock Holmes, this is James Hastings, one of the finest goalies I have ever had the honor to serve."

"I must say, Watson, seeing you again is the first good

thing to happen to me in days," said he.

"Pray take a seat and give us the reason for your visit to our humble quarters," said Holmes as I placed a kettle on the Bunsen burner for tea. "Please do not spare a single detail."

"It's my sister, Charlotte," said Hastings, who nervously smoothed his black moustache throughout the interview. "You've heard of that horrible panic in Spitalfields earlier this week, of course. I believe my sister, Charlotte, was in attendance, and now she is missing."

"Your sister speaks Hebrew?" Holmes asked.

"Yes, sir. Charlotte is quite plain, and has always had a severe demeanor. She never married, and has spent her life busying herself with church matters. She has adopted the Spitalfields district as her hunting ground for lost souls. She tries to covert the Jews and foreigners to Christianity through charitable works. Setting a Christian example, one might say. To this end, she learned their heathen speech. "

"When did you last hear from her?" asked Holmes.

"On Saturday. Charlotte usually spends the Sabbath with the rest of the family. It's somewhat of a Hastings tradition."

"Did anything seem unusual?"

"Not in the slightest. She brought us up to date on her doings, and told us she intended to see this comedy at the dramatic club. That's how I know she was there."

"Perhaps she attended to something else."

"She hasn't been seen since that night."

"Surely the regular police can make enquiries."

"They are doing so, but they also have to contend with more immediate concerns, petty crime of all types, and drunken ruffians. I do not feel they are giving this the proper attention."

"Pray tell me what you know about her mission."

"She calls on Jewish families in need to see if she can offer her assistance. If she sees a sick child, she'll find a doctor. If they're in need of food, she will procure a meal. She asks, in return, that they read her tracts and the Christian Bible, and she tries to get them into the Christian church, of course."

"Does she have enemies?"

"She has had encounters with husbands who don't like outsiders meddling with family affairs, but nothing to provoke violence, at least so far as she has told me."

"How about it, Holmes?" I prompted.

"There is little in this case to pique my interest," said Holmes, his eye drifting toward the syringe he keeps in a velvet case. "She may simply have had enough of life among the wretched and taken off for a respite. She will no doubt turn up on the morrow, just in time for dinner."

"Holmes, may I have a word?"

We stepped over to the window.

"Your reliance on the seven percent solution to relieve your boredom is starting to take its toll," I said. "You've barely eaten in days, and I can see the early signs of malnutrition. You also haven't seen daylight since Tuesday. You need air and exercise. For your own good, get out of this flat and give my old friend some reassurance."

Turning our attention back to our guest, Holmes proffered a cigarette and lit one himself.

"The good doctor has persuaded me," Holmes said with a genial smile. "I am delighted to take up the case."

"There's a temporary morgue at the club on Princes' Street," Hastings said. "You haven't long; Mr. Baxter is releasing the bodies to the families so they may honor the Jewish custom of burial before the second day after death."

"Your sister is not among them?"

"No, but she may still be inside the entertainment hall.

I don't know whether there has been a thorough search."

Holmes nodded. "Watson? Are you game?"

"Every time, my good fellow."

Spitalfields is one of London's poverty capitals: overcrowded, smelly even for the city, infested with all sorts of vermin, miserable sanitation, crammed with foreigners, mostly Jews, who have come here to escape even worse conditions in their original homes. Hastings took us down Brick Lane to a narrow brick thoroughfare which turned out to be Princes' Street, stopping at No. 3, the dwelling which masked a theatre capable of accommodating some 500 people, according to Mr. A. Smith, the theatre's manager. I should place Smith's age as about ten years older than myself, his high forehead topped with thick, black and somewhat curly hair. A heavy brush moustache drew attention to his bulbous nose. I'd say he stood a head shorter than Holmes.

"This woman," Holmes said, showing Smith the photograph Hastings had provided. "Do you know if she was in the audience?"

"Sister Hastings? Of course she was here. She frequently attended our events. She saw it as an opportunity to preach her evangel."

"Have you accounted for everyone present?" Holmes asked.

"We have accounted for all the dead ones," Smith replied. "You'd have to ask the police about anyone else."

"Did you find any indication that someone may have caused the panic deliberately?"

"Not to my eye. I can't imagine who might gain from something like this, except perhaps a deranged prankster."

"So you don't know if Sister Hastings escaped."

"Nor do I know she didn't. But she was not among the dead. Of that I am certain."

"May we take a look inside?"

"Please do."

Those who constructed this theatre had done a splendid job. One upper tier of benches served the balcony crowd, while wooden chairs, most now overturned and broken, served the rest. A small orchestra pit kept the crowd separate from the stage, at the moment hidden by the large and heavy purple curtain.

"Mr. Holmes, if you can find any clues in this mess, my hat's off to you," Hastings said.

"We won't learn much here," Holmes said in agreement, "but we haven't seen everything. Watson, go ask Smith if he knows where the gas was cut off, will you?"

We found the meter behind the stage, and some strange-looking finger marks in the dust on the cutoff switch. Whoever did this had extremely slender and very long fingers with sharp nails.

"Hmmm," grunted Holmes. "I've never seen such marks before, and there is no doubt this was done deliberately. These marks do not look like a man's fingers, yet what else could they be? What purpose could possibly have been served?"

"Perhaps someone wanted to cover up another situation," I suggested.

"Possibly. If so, then it is also possible that Sister Hastings was the target of kidnappers. If they rushed her out of here in the panic, they would look like rescuers and no one would suspect otherwise until too late. Very good. You have possibilities, Watson."

The stage, of course, had not been struck, so all the furniture, props, and other accoutrements of the play were still in place. Cursing the dimness, Holmes ignored Hastings and me as he went about his peculiar ritual of tape measurements, subtle muttering, and magnifying glass for the next twenty minutes or so.

A quick movement in the corner of my eye drew my attention to an uncommonly large rat over in the corner, by the stage right entrance. I could not suppress a shudder. To be honest, rats frighten me. I have sickening memories of rat packs dining on corpses left too long on the battlefield, a genuinely revolting sight. Sometimes those memories haunt my nightmares, and my stomach always curdles whenever I encounter one.

This devilish creature, about the size of a cat, seemed to be observing the scene, and I would swear that, if it could, it would have been taking notes. The creature eyed us with a malevolent curiosity and unnatural intelligence, its eyes red, wide and curious. My spine ran cold when it saw me looking at it. Our eyes met, and I could swear the creature seemed to be trying to memorize my face, displaying an unusual, near-human interest in its spiteful expression. Then it looked away and skittered over to the stage right entrance.

I followed it, keeping my distance. Down below the stage it went, and under the door to one of the dressing rooms. I had my hand on the knob to follow when I heard a stern Holmes bark, "Watson! What do you think you're doing? Don't disturb those rooms!"

"This may be important!" I snapped back.

Holmes rushed down the stairs, followed by Hastings, and we let Holmes enter the room first.

"We'll need a lantern, or at least get the gas going again," said Holmes. "My, it's stuffy down here. Watson, what did you deem so urgent?"

"A huge and nasty-looking rat, Holmes. Like nothing I've ever seen. It seemed to have sentience. It seems to have been studying us. Nasty brute."

"And what might it have to do with our case?"

"For all I know, nothing, but—"

"While I appreciate your natural curiosity, Doctor, I

find it unlikely that our missing evangelist was kidnapped by mammoth rats and dragged into the catacombs of London. Let's look for something a little more prosaic, shall we?"

Once the light was restored, we were able to examine the room, and we found nothing to indicate that Sister Hastings had ever set foot in it. We did find a five-inch hole in the wainscoting and some droppings, no doubt the rat's (or is it rats'?) point of entry.

"We should alert Mr. Smith at once," I said. "There is no more efficient spreader of disease than the average city rat."

"At least something worthwhile will come from this, then," said Holmes. "I daresay, Mr. Hastings, that your sister at least made it out of the theatre alive. We must find her trail elsewhere."

"I must take my leave of you," Hastings said when we left the premises. "I do have a business requiring my attention. It was good to see you again, Watson. We must find a pub and catch up sometime. Mr. Holmes, you'll keep me apprised of your progress?"

"Of course," Holmes replied, shaking Hastings' hand. "A pleasure."

From there, we made our way to the tenement where Sister Hastings made her home. As Holmes and I walked the narrow, cobbled streets, I again had the unearthly feeling of being watched. I noticed nothing suspicious about the people around us, the usual polyglot of foreign tradesmen, drunkards, drab housewives, thieves, and unaccompanied children. Yet, in the corner of my eye, the street creatures, the rodents, appeared to be everywhere – peering at us from alleys, from holes in walls, from the windows of empty apartments, their whiskers twitching as if sending signals. They seemed to know who we were, and they gave me every impression of being tracked. I felt uncomfortably like prey in the jungle. A feeling of nausea swept through me.

"Let's not spend too much time in this place," I told Holmes. "I truly dislike it here."

"I'm not having a pleasant time myself, Doctor, but you are the one who put me on this case."

"Work your miracles, Holmes, just work your miracles."

Sister Hastings lived in a soot-covered and generally filthy brick building, where at least she had a room to herself. We spent perhaps an hour interviewing her neighbors, who generally agreed she had attended the play that night, and that she hadn't been seen since. An inspection of her rooms turned up little.

"She writes tracts under the name of C.M. Hastings," Holmes observed after rifling her desk. "She seems particularly keen on creation and God's relationship with the natural world. She sees the hand of God in every affair, natural and human. In her current effort, she asks, 'What Does God Want from Us?' Also, there's a list of people she intended to visit this week. A few sick children and a mother raising three siblings on her own. Of course, she belongs to a temperance society, and is due to speak to them tomorrow."

"Will you attend?"

"I may. But I'll brace myself at a pub first."

We heard a knock at the door. A small lad, undernourished, his age about ten, stepped inside.

"Are you looking for Sister Hastings?" he asked.

"We are," I said. "Do you know where she is?"

"No, but you're not the first one. There was another man in here yesterday."

"Really?" said Holmes. "Do you know who?"

The boy shook his head.

"He was short and fat," he said. "He was bent over her desk, and he wore a grey fur coat."

"Did you get a look at his face?"

Again, the boy shook his head.

"It was pretty dark," he said. "I saw a little of his face from the street lamp. He had a long and sharp nose."

"He didn't remind you of a huge rat, did he?" I asked.

"That's it!" the boy cried. "He looked just like a big rat, but he moved like a man. Rats don't really get that big, do they?"

"How big was this one?" Holmes asked.

"About an inch or two taller than me," the boy said. "Really heavy. At least nine stone, maybe more."

"What's your name, boy?" Holmes asked.

"Isaac Perelberg, sir."

"Here's a shilling, Isaac, and my business card. If you see Sister Hastings again, or the strange man, then you should get in touch with me at once."

"Will there be more shillings for me?"

"Yes."

"Thank you, sir!"

Now Holmes returned to his examinations, and looked around the room one more time. His face had paled by the time he finished.

"Holmes, what is it?"

"Not here, Watson. We need a cab immediately."

As we rode back into our part of the city, Holmes remained mute and would not entertain any of my questions until we found a pub on Northumberland Street. Not until we had two good pints of beer in front of us did my friend finally relax.

"Well, Holmes, why the mystery?"

"What is my maxim, Watson?"

"'When you eliminated the impossible, whatever remains, however improbable, must be the truth.' So what is the truth?"

14

"I found rat droppings the size of industrial ball bearings on the floor of Sister Hastings' room. In other words, your theory has taken on a great deal of plausibility."

"You know more than you're letting on, aren't you?"

Holmes sighed.

"I suppose I'd better tell you the whole story, but not until we go back home. The world is not ready for what I am about to share with you."

From the Journals of George Edward Challenger, assistant lecturer, Largs Academy, Edinburgh University

January 1887

Blessing or curse?

I have been dismissed from my position as assistant lecturer at Largs Academy, where I suffered under the tutelage of lesser lights before my escape to University. A severe deficiency of funds forced me back here to lecture on the biological sciences to bored, ignorant adolescents whose minds would rather run to the insubstantial pleasures of sport and sexual fantasy than to the miracles that lay at their fingertips through the wonder and bounty of Nature. They have eyes, but they refuse to see beyond the tips of their endlessly running noses.

I know I have the potential to join the ranks of the great zoological researchers, if only I could find an opportunity. Yet that opportunity consistently eludes my grasp, for no better reason than my inability to flash empty smiles, assuage egos, or tolerate error. How is science to advance if its most prominent practitioners are locked in hidebound conclusion and empty conformity? This cannot be the path to truth, and yet the intolerant fools who populate our scientific circles refuse to either see or listen to anyone who doesn't ape their preferred forms of behavior. How can one understand the ocean if one can't rock the boat on occasion?

Though today's events will leave me penniless unless things change soon, perhaps there is a way to see this as a prospect. For though my funds are low, my time is now abundant: my plans to return to University this autumn are still in place, and there is time to secure a position elsewhere, perhaps closer to London. As I have been ejected from my rooms on campus, perhaps I should take it as a signal from Fate that I head south to the great city and join the teeming millions making their lives at the heart of the Empire.

I shall wire Quintus Jones, my friend, colleague and curator of the University's science museum in London. He should be able to guide me.

The curse is the blessing!

Jones has directed me to cheap quarters near the university, where my fellow students fester when they are here. Once I settled in, he was kind enough to invite me to dinner, prepared by his charming wife, Marjorie.

On first meeting, they seem an unlikely couple: Jones is tall and slender, yet graceful, while Marjorie is clearly of peasant stock; she is shorter than he by nearly a foot, her body that of a farmer's wife, but fair of face. Indeed, her hair, her best feature, complements her face with a perfect frame as she stares up at Jones with adoring eyes. He, in turn, smiles down on her with benevolence and love. No wonder they have five children. Thank God none of them happened to be present when I came by.

"They're playing in the nursery," Jones said as he shook my hand in greeting.

"Thank you for thinking of it."

"Had they met you, I'm sure they would be thanking me. What brings you from the wilds of Scotland, Challenger?"

We settled in the parlor and lit cigars. Marjorie poured whiskies for us, splashing a bit of water into her husband's glass.

"Two semesters," Jones said. "A record for you. I thought you'd be gone after the first."

"What can I say, Jones? I simply am not fit to lecture dull-witted boys who no more want my attention than I want

17

to waste it. It's like pouring water into a bucket with a large hole. I am taking this latest dismissal as an opportunity to alter my circumstances and find a better path."

"Fortune may be smiling on you in that regard," said Jones. "I have here a letter from my brother Sixtus, who is a social reformer in the East End. He resides among the foreign Jews of Spitalfields, who have been put to a panic by large animals."

"Animals, you say?"

Jones handed me the letter, and said, "Read the second paragraph, will you?"

I saw that the handwriting was every bit as neat and legible as that of Quintus, a curious family trait. I read the letter aloud:

"'I am sorry to report that my efforts to bring about better housing conditions for the residents of Spitalfields have been derailed of late due to rumors of giant rodents being spotted in the neighborhood. As the stories grow wilder, so does the fear, and I am anxious to do something before it goes out of control. I am told these creatures are the size of a small man, covered in either grey or brown fur, and have glowing red eyes. One of our Christian sisters has gone missing, and the gossip mill has her as a prisoner of these monsters, as if they exist. Personally, Quint, I think a wombat escaped from the zoological park, but nonetheless, the neighborhood discusses nothing else, rendering my efforts to improve their lot useless of late.'"

I handed the letter back.

"What do you expect me to do about this?"

"Capture one, Challenger. Bring one in for study. Perhaps some exotic new species of rodent has made its way to the streets of London from the Orient. Perhaps there has been some unusual mutation or cross-breeding resulting in a new and stronger species of rat. Or it may be pranksters in fur coats. You told me you had means for about a month, is that right?"

"That's the sad truth of it."

"I'll stake your researches," Jones said, the smoke rising slowly and majestically from his cigar, giving him a slightly regal air. "If the long shot pays off and there is a new species of rodent under the streets, I daresay you will finally be feted in the way you always wanted, and I will share in the spoils for working with you on this most interesting project. Who knows? We may win the Crayston itself."

I am ashamed to say my eyes lit up too quickly. Jones laughed.

"You're young and hungry, Challenger. You have plenty of time to establish a career. I am halfway through mine, and I have children and a wife to feed. There are many things I regret not doing because I started a family so soon, and perhaps I'm helping you now to make up for that. Sharing in a prestigious prize can only boost my own prospects. We both benefit if you're successful."

A new species: perhaps the last surviving members of rodents long thought extinct, like the giant hutia. Either way, Jones was right. It shouldn't take a month to find and capture one. Two, ideally, one for observation and one for dissection.

"Jones, you have persuaded me," said I. "Tomorrow I find your brother, and the giant rat hunt is on. Release the hounds!"

We both laughed, and refreshed our whiskies.

Sixtus Jones proved to be a stout man, several years older than his leaner brother, but every bit as keen. It surprised me to learn that their father had taught biology at Oxford in times past.

"You should have been a scientist, like your brother," I told him.

Sixtus shook his head.

"I was good at that sort of thing, even enjoyed it after a fashion, but the problems of society are immense, and few are stepping forward to solve them. I went through a period of poverty when I was younger, and it opened my eyes like nothing else could. You don't want that experience, Mr. Challenger. I have devoted my life to eradicating poverty, to the extent that one can."

"So you chose housing."

"Just so, sir, just so. The first step to a decent life is a decent home."

"Appropriately, we have rats to catch. Here's what I have in mind."

I outlined my approach: once Jones supplied me with a list of sightings and their locations, I would then make a map and plant traps: specifically, I would use roasted nuts as lures. The difficult bit would be devising a trap of sufficient size and strength.

"Why nuts?" Jones asked.

"Because they are nutritious and salty," I said. "Some of my colleagues use them to reward their own lab rats when their performance has been exceptional."

"Clever."

"I know."

Using Jones's information, I narrowed the creature sightings to a radius of about three city blocks in the neighborhood of Spitalfields. But first, we needed some proper traps.

Between my students and the laboratory, I am more than familiar with rodent behavior. I decided on a spring trap. I would prepare a room with a single entrance, and place the bait on a table just beyond the door. Once my quarry stepped on the trigger (a steel plate under the rug), bars would drop, blocking the exit. In case the beastie proved supple, I interwove chains between the bars, rendering escape impossible for any but the smallest and most flexible of rodents.

Now, the location. After the first few proved less than worthy, I came upon the Hebrew Club theatre, and its manager, one Mr. Smith, a harried man badly in need of a good barber. Jones told me one of the creatures was seen there and may have contributed to the recent and deadly panic.

"We are still recovering from the stampede," Smith told me, "but you can use our green room, if you like."

"Green room? Do you grow flowers in there?"

"It's theatre argot, Mr. Challenger. It's where actors await their cues to take the stage. Ours isn't exactly green. We did it up in blue wallpaper to make the actors more comfortable and at home. They're nervous enough as it is."

I'll say this for Smith; he could not have provided a better venue for my plan. The size of an office large enough to hold a desk, chair and file cabinet, it had several wooden chairs, a sofa, and a table with an elaborate cut glass ashtray at its center.

"Capital, Mr. Smith, capital. I'll send the workmen in as soon as I assemble the materials. When do you anticipate reopening the theatre?"

"Not for at least a month. We're still selecting plays at present."

"With luck, our plans won't take that long."

I had always thought of Jews as skilled craftsmen, but I did not count on the Babel of different languages the crew brought to the task. Even those proficient in the Hebrew tongue had differing accents, which meant the wrong tools were sometimes used, instructions untranslated or unheeded altogether, and the poor ventilation meant their taking a number of breaks just to get fresh air; that is, if you can call the wretched reek of the unsanitary streets of Spitalfields to be "fresh." A job which should have taken no more than two days ran instead to five. Next time, I'm bringing hard-headed and practical Scotsmen in. They know how to get a job done.

When I was finally satisfied, I showed Jones my handiwork.

"Well done, Mr. Challenger! It looks no different."

"It took some time, but we got there. Take a look inside."

Jones stepped into the room, and the gate came down with a satisfying crash. Startled, Jones must have jumped half a foot.

"Challenger! That wasn't funny!"

I thought it quite amusing, and could not suppress a solid horse laugh.

"My apologies, sir, but I had to know how well it worked."

"You have your answer, dammit! Get me out of here!"

I opened a panel in the wall and winched the gate back up. Jones, looking no worse for my little joke, stepped back out, just as Smith arrived to take a look.

"This is excellent, if I may say so," he said. "Now I know where to put unruly actors."

"Not to mention harsh critics," said I. "Tonight, we set the trap."

By now, I knew where the creatures were getting in; one of the dressing rooms underneath the stage. The pattern of rat droppings showed where they foraged, and that included the green room. It made sense; often, the actors would sup there before and during performances.

As I feared, the first four nights passed with no luck, but, when I arrived on the fifth morning, I heard a frightful clamor.

"I say! Help! Get me out!"

My stomach sank. Rats are quite intelligent, but I have

yet to encounter one with the power of speech. Imagine my surprise when I saw Smith peering through a small gap in the chains.

"Mr. Smith, what the devil are you doing in there?"

"I heard something before going home last night. I saw one!"

"What? Did you get a good look? Where were you?"

"I was coming out of my office when I heard something move in the theatre. Of course I came down to look, and I saw it! About four feet high, a stubby pink tail, and bright devil's eyes which caught me in their sight. Revolting creature! I don't mind admitting I screamed. I panicked and ran into the green room without thinking. I never want to see such an apparition again."

"My God, man! Did the creature see you?"

"It scurried offstage when I screamed. I'm afraid I have bungled your plans, Mr. Challenger."

"Perhaps not. Let's see what we can see."

"I have an idea," said Smith. "One reason we have problems with rats is our proximity to the sewage system. You know this area, Mr. Jones. They get in everywhere. Perhaps it might be as well to not only bait this trap, but to find some means of tracking them to their lair. These beasts are simply too large to disappear into the walls. They have to have a larger means of ingress."

"They still have the flexible spines of their smaller kindred," I reminded him. "They may only need a few inches for their crawling space."

"It's still larger than the average hole in the wall. I submit they've been using the workmen's crawling spaces under the street."

"I still want to capture one," I reminded him.

"You still have to find them first," Smith said. "I should have thought of this sooner."

Smith directed us to the nearest manhole, which was located on the main thoroughfare nearby. Using one of the theatre's lanterns, it took about half an hour to find the rodents' main trail.

"Thank you, Mr. Smith," I said, "this will save us a considerable amount of time. We'll return here tonight. I'll leave plenty of the roasted nuts where the rodents can find them, and we'll follow them at a safe distance. Be sure to arm yourself, Mr. Jones. We may need protection if they prove to be dangerous."

"Arm myself? Do you mean a gun, Challenger?"

"Only as a precaution, Jones, only as a precaution."

Dr. Watson's Journal

January 22, 1887

Sherlock Holmes has just related to me one of the most remarkable stories I have ever heard, and, if it's true, a grand villain may well have returned to the world.

After breakfast this morning, Holmes handed me a sensational pamphlet. A photograph of an extremely strange creature, a freakish and repellent blending of dog and rat, stared at me with great, toothsome malice.

Underneath the photograph, the title read, "The Moreau Horrors, an Investigation into Madness and Monstrosity."

"You are the first person to hear what I am about to tell," Holmes said, pouring us fresh cups of coffee. "What I tell you must never reach the public prints. The world may never be fully prepared for the truth about Dr. Alexandre Moreau."

I opened my notebook, pen in hand.

"I mean it, Watson. Don't be too hasty. I must insist you keep this story quiet until I give you permission to publish."

"I understand, Holmes."

"Very well, then."

Holmes lit his first cigarette of the day and began:

The public has mostly forgotten these events in the past ten years, but they are engraved upon my memory forever. The curious chain of events which led to Dr. Moreau's exile helped set me on my current path. You may recall my having created a reagent which can identify blood when first we met. Had the events I am about to relate not occurred, I might never have performed that work, and, indeed, you would be rooming with a very different man.

I digress. Of course you remember Langdale Pike.

"That bounder! He's a gossip monger. The lowest form of journalist."

Also a chum from University, which is where this remarkable tale begins. I was not long graduated and, desperately in need of funds, took a position in the University's chemistry department, where one afternoon, a breathless Pike sent an urgent note asking me to meet him at the local pub on a warm summer evening.

You only know the successful Pike, Watson, not the struggling journalist looking to make a name for himself. Unsuccessful at finding a post on Fleet Street, Pike began to accept single assignments from any editor who would give him one. The night I met him, he seemed almost breathless with fright and anxiety.

"What is it, Pike? You reek of fear."

"Holmes, I need help, and of everyone I know only you have the knowledge and discretion necessary."

"Discretion? An odd word, coming from you."

"I need an independent witness to support what I expect to write, for on my own, no one will believe it."

"And, in return?"

"All I can offer is the satisfaction of seeing justice done and evil stopped cold. Once I verify what I have been told, of course. If you're working for me, you're working for beer. But if the articles I have in mind make the splash I think they will, you would have entrée to some of the greatest laboratories in Europe."

Pike revealed he had heard disturbing rumors about the most mysterious man on campus, the aforementioned Dr. Alexandre Moreau. At the time, Moreau was a biologist and zoologist of some note, and it was long rumored he sought the sort of breakthroughs which could unravel the very mysteries of life itself. I knew of him through his blood research: he claimed to be on the path of universal blood transfusion, which, Doctor, you must admit would be a boon to your profession.

"What's more important is that his assistant has departed without warning. No one has seen hide or hair of the man in days. Dark rumors are circulating, Holmes, very dark rumors indeed."

My curiosity piqued, I asked Pike what he wanted me to do.

"Dr. Moreau is looking for a new laboratory assistant," said Pike. "I would like you to apply, and to report back to me every day of the goings-on in the laboratory. You may have to endure some extremely distasteful experiences."

"It would be an honor to be accepted. Universal transfusion might be worth some unpleasantness."

"Not if the rumors I have heard prove to be true. Pray keep a precise journal, and meet me here once a week at about this time to share what you have seen. No one has an eye for details or a memory such as yours, Holmes. It should be put to the betterment of mankind rather than mortifying young women and embarrassing your classmates."

"Noted. Assuming I take the position."

"Can you afford this meal we're enjoying?"

"Barely, Pike. Barely."

"Nothing motivates a search for employment like hunger. Let's meet here in a week at this time."

I tell you, Watson, the interview left me both excited and nervous. I could have my name associated with one of the greatest medical discoveries of the nineteenth century. Or there could be some sinister secret, assuming Pike was right. One could not say Pike's natural gifts lay in the sciences.

Pike's evasive manner about his suspicions of Moreau

concerned me deeply, and I was inclined to dismiss them. He has a tendency to exaggerate for the purpose of sensationalism, and he did not share any specific information about what he had heard, except that Moreau may have been mistreating his lab animals.

Besides, there could be any number of perfectly reasonable explanations for the lab assistant to leave his position suddenly; trouble in the family, an irresistible new opportunity, a culminating romance. Perhaps he found Moreau an unpleasant taskmaster. His departure seemed to me of little importance.

I found my heart beating a bit faster when I met the man himself for the first time. At that point in my life, I had not encountered anyone so imposing on first meeting. Alexandre Moreau commanded the room. A powerfully built man of about fifty, his shock of white hair made him appear somewhat godlike. He had a fine forehead, and thick features, particularly the whitish lips and an aquiline Romanesque nose, which gave him a powerful impression of being resolute, fearless, and, especially, unopposed in any venture he should wish to undertake.

The faint aroma of chemicals marked Moreau as a scientist right away, and his fading tan and tribal signet ring told me, among other things, that he had traveled in jungle climes recently. His perfectly tailored clothing and fitted shoes spoke of family wealth; no one could afford such finery on a professor's salary. Such a man would not easily make friends, and, indeed, he eyed me with suspicion.

He took my slender hand in a massive paw and gave it a painful squeeze before indicating a chair.

"So, Mr. Sherlock Holmes," he said. "I have made enquiries among your professors, and it is said you have the potential to be the finest scientist of your generation. Why tie yourself to me?"

28

"I have heard rumors of a potential breakthrough regarding blood transfusions. Some claim you may have discovered the secret of life itself. I further heard that your previous assistant seems to have disappeared."

"Ah, that," Moreau said with a shrug. "Some men simply don't have the stomach for true science. As to the secret of life itself, that, sir, is pure hyperbole, though it is true that some of my research has shown promise. Still, it is odd your name had not reached me before now. I'm told you have an interest in justice, as well?"

"I have taken an interest in some cases in the penny press," I told him. "They are not without interest to the scientist."

"Indeed. Would you use what you have learned here for that purpose?"

"I don't see how I could. I have no desire to be a policeman, Dr. Moreau. The mysteries of biochemistry are far more enchanting to me."

"I have many applicants to consider, Mr. Holmes. Do a small demonstration for me, and we'll see if you have what it takes to advance."

He led me to a small laboratory, and had me do some basic work: identifying micro-organisms, creating common chemical reactions, and the like. He also had me perform a somewhat advanced biochemical experiment; luckily, one with which I was already familiar.

"You do your work in a clean and efficient manner," said he. "It speaks well of you. I will let you know."

To my surprise, Watson, he did accept me. My eyes filled with wonder on the very first day. Doctor Moreau had lab equipment unlike any I had ever encountered before, and, I learned later, most of it had been specifically engineered according to his specifications. He had centrifuges, equipment for electrolysis, spectrometry, and much, much more. I confess to instant admiration and an eagerness to get started. I had little to tell Pike that first week.

"I've been feeding lab animals and preparing chemicals," I said. "Dr. Moreau has yet to tell me what any of them are, though I recognize some basic components of the bloodstream. He uses a great deal of saline. I suspect the Doctor is not a trusting man."

"Have you seen him performing any experiments on dogs?"

"I have heard some howling from the private lab where no one but Moreau sets foot."

"That's where you must go, Holmes. Whatever Dr. Moreau's secret is, it has to be in there."

"He keeps the door locked and the key to himself."

"You won't let that deter you, I hope."

I nearly left Pike right at the table.

"I said I'd report to you, but I'm no burglar!" I snapped. "If there is ever anything to report, I promise you I shall report it. I'll not do more!"

I see you smiling, Watson. I was less a man of the world then.

My second private interview with Moreau occurred the Monday following.

"I have been most impressed with you, young Sherlock Holmes. Though I have given you the most menial of tasks, you have not only performed them with the skill and assurance of a master, you have also not raised a single word of complaint. I believe I may trust you, but you must promise to keep what you learn here to yourself. I have no wish to announce anything to the world until I am absolutely sure. If I am correct, you will share in the accolades, perhaps even the Crayston Prize for Zoological Research. Can I trust you?"

"Insofar as the experiments fall within ethical boundaries and produce tangible results, then I am your man."

Moreau smiled and said, "We may have to press some ethical boundaries a bit, but if we are successful, the results will be worth it."

I did not know, Watson, what was to transpire. At that point, I decided to tell Pike his suspicions were groundless and to find another assignment. That would change. Besides, I needed the job.

Though Moreau said he had decided to trust me, it soon became clear he had not made up his mind about me yet. We ran a standard laboratory operation, focusing on blood research. We conducted experiments on the usual animals: rats, squirrels, stray pets, anything we could scour from the streets of London. Week after week went by with nothing unusual, though I daresay the average Londoner might have felt queasy watching us work.

But I did not spend all my time with Moreau, and I knew he was hiding something from me. Sometimes he would leave the outer laboratory to me for hours on end as he labored in his private lab. Often, he would take my research in with him. This, I'm sad to say now, flattered me.

After a month, I told Pike I had no reason to suspect Dr. Moreau of anything more than a few imperfect laboratory practices and the eccentricities not uncommon to men of genius. But not long after that, I had occasion to return to the lab after work, having left my boarding house key in my smock. As I was about to leave, a blood-curdling screech cut through the air, the cry of a wounded and dangerous animal, and it came from the private lab. When I heard Moreau's voice, I ran to help. But he'd locked the door, Watson.

"Doctor Moreau!" I cried, pounding on the door. "Are you all right?"

No answer, just another hideous animal shriek. I thrust my shoulder against the door until the wood cracked and gave way, almost spilling me onto the floor.

The sight which greeted my eye would have moved the most hardened heart. Row after row of cages with strange creatures which suggested the chimeras of Greek myth – rats with the nimble agility of squirrels, strange cat-dog hybrids, animals which seemed to have been created not through husbandry, but through assembly. Many seemed to have merged into new and unique creatures over the passage of time. The wretched beasts were covered with stitches; heads did not match bodies, and all glared at me with equal expressions of fear, anger, and hatred.

Another scream shook me back to reality and the situation at hand. I rushed to the source of that hideous sound, to find Moreau doing something vile to a pair of fully conscious cats. They hissed and cried, their agony reaching to the heavens as, immobile, they could do nothing but endure the torture inflicted on them by the man I suddenly realized had to be cruel, if not in the neighborhood of madness.

Moreau's head snapped around and caught me in a cold, disdainful glare.

"I thought you had left for the day," he said.

"What are you doing to those poor, innocent creatures?" I demanded.

"I am testing their tolerance for pain. I can hardly do that if they are anaesthetized."

"What are those creatures in the cages?"

Moreau smiled with the cold calculation of a cobra.

"Perhaps the greatest of scientific discoveries," he said. "Surely the betterment of mankind is worth the pitiful howling of a few unwanted animals?"

"Does the University know what you're doing in here? They'll take their money back for—"

"The University has nothing to say about it. I come from a wealthy family, Mr. Holmes. They have interests all over the world. I rent these facilities with my own funds, even though the University will certainly claim some credit once my research is complete."

"Nevertheless, I shall—"

"I should hope you give me the benefit of the doubt until I am in a better position to explain. As you can see, I am a bit preoccupied at the moment. We shall have tea tomorrow morning. You said I could trust you, Mr. Holmes."

"Within the bounds of ethics," I replied.

"Yes. We shall have a chat about that. I beg your indulgence until eight o'clock tomorrow. Now, good night."

With that, he turned his back to me and continued tormenting the cats with no more care or concern than if he were gutting a freshly caught fish. I caught a glint of light on his scalpel before I left the lab.

As I made my way back through the private lab, I noticed more specially engineered laboratory equipment, of the sort found only in the most advanced biological laboratories, and some equipment well beyond my competence. The blood research we conducted during the day was somehow being transmuted into something else. Something which enabled Moreau to physically assemble living creatures, perhaps with an eye to …

The thought of human experimentation in such a dark and mysterious place as this knotted my stomach, and I badly needed fresh air. I went to a pub and nursed a couple of whiskies trying to determine what I should do, eventually deciding that the man deserved a chance to explain. But I slept poorly that night, Watson, I'll tell you that.

When I returned to the lab the following morning, the pleasant aroma of freshly brewed tea and French pastry just out of the oven greeted my nostrils, and I followed the scent to Moreau's office, as neat, tidy, and organized as his laboratory. His desk and furniture all constructed of oak and mahogany, hard and dark woods reflecting the soul of the man himself. He had dressed, not in his usual work attire, but in a black frock coat and tie, as befits a professor about to give a lecture.

"Mr. Sherlock Holmes," the doctor said. "You have honored me by your presence. If I am successful, I shall persuade you to join me on a great adventure, an adventure no other scientist has ever pursued, despite the materials laying before him in clear daylight."

He handed me a cup of tea as I sat down, getting the amount of milk I prefer exactly right. The fact that Moreau knew this without asking pricked my ears; he had been observing me as closely as I had been observing him. This also meant he might have powers of observation to rival my own. I wondered if he knew about my arrangement with Pike.

We did not discuss the topic at hand straightaway. Moreau sought to put me at my ease before beginning, setting the stage properly to achieve the singular effect he sought for his audience of one. Only when we shared cigars did he at last address my concerns.

"Did I ever tell you the singular factor which won you your position?" he asked. "Your fingers. You have the fingers of a skilled surgeon. I imagine the violin keeps them nimble."

"How did you know I play the violin?"

Moreau smiled.

"The lingering scent of rosin gives you away. But we aren't here to discuss music. How familiar are you with surgery?"

"I have a layman's knowledge." Remember, Watson, I was not long out of school.

"Then you may not be familiar with skin grafts. Say a man has burned his face. It is possible to slice some fresh skin from, say, the thigh, and place it over the burns. Given time, the skin will grow and become healthy, as if never burned at all, save for some unavoidable scarring.

"It is the same with vivisection. We can graft skin and flesh, we can graft bone. If we can do this, must we stop there? Can we not graft between different animals of the same species? Of different species?"

"That is not possible by any science I understand," said I.

"Quite correct. Not science you understand. My journey began with the blood research upon which I have employed your talents. Once we have solved the problem of universal transfusion, much more is possible. We are very close, Mr. Holmes. Very close indeed."

"Then those hideous creatures in your lab—"

"Have accepted and adapted my formula, yes. Which has allowed me to alter them, and their very natures."

"Can you not use anesthetic for your operations? Why must those animals suffer?"

"I do not wish to pollute their blood with unnatural chemicals, and I wish to learn the nature of pain. Since pain is an inevitable consequence of my work, I see no reason not to add it to my researches. Much benefit to humanity may result. Suppose, just suppose, Mr. Holmes, that we learn enough about pain to change its nature? To make it possible for a man to learn of damage to his body in some way other than making him suffer? Again, we may be on the road to great things.

"What, precisely, is pain? Only a means of alerting the body to an event requiring its urgent attention. Not all flesh feels pain, not even every sensory nerve. A wound to the optic nerve results in a change of vision, but no pain. Plants do not feel pain, nor the lowest animals. Besides, the body bears no memory of pain. And the animal becomes disciplined. Control the animal's chemistry, and controlling its body will follow."

I could not let this pass without reply.

"The body retains no memory of the pain itself," I said, "but does not forget the experience of pain. A man administered morphine for a broken leg will not forget the reason he was given morphine when the drug wears off."

"Yet that same man may develop a tolerance for a certain level of pain, perhaps even to the point where it may not matter if he feels pain."

"You are unmoved by the animals' suffering?"

"In the betterment of the human race, I must suppress my natural sympathies, of course."

"What happens once you have solved the problem of universal transfusion?"

"It remains important, and we will continue, but my journey has taken me down a different path. I now know it is possible to transplant tissue from one part of an animal to another, and even to a completely different animal. In time, I'll be able to change its most intimate structure. Universal transfusion will only make my work proceed more quickly, if I am successful. The Moreau family, of course, will control the patents. I am no philanthropist.

"Look to your history, Mr. Holmes. Medieval practitioners, for example, created creatures we now enjoy as freaks in a sideshow. Victor Hugo gives an account of some of them in *L'Homme qui Rit*. In my researches so far, it seems as if I have this particular branch of science all to myself."

"Yet what you are doing is monstrous. Universal transfusion would be a huge benefit to mankind. Why not stop there? That alone would make your name immortal."

"Because there is so much more knowledge to be gained. Imagine what I could accomplish if I am successful. Cripples able to walk again, the feeble rendered intelligent, the deformed made whole. Universal transfusion is but the beginning. Much of what we already know comes as the result of unintended consequences, actions by criminals and tyrants, animal breeders, and by sheer accident. Using modern science, we need not blunder about in the dark. We can take a measured and paced path to what, ultimately, could be human perfection. A master race, if you will."

"What you're saying sounds quite—"

"Mad? Some might think so. Yet, my historical researches have found indications that I am not the first, but only the first to try to do these things properly. Take the Inquisition. The Inquisitors' intent was to use torment to obtain information, but there must have been some scientific curiosity. They must have learned something, and I have found that they did."

Moreau said these shocking things as if they were the most normal of scientific practices, as if those poor animals' pain and suffering meant nothing at all. I was a more sensitive soul then, Watson, and Moreau's calm demeanor made everything he said seem somehow worse. All that mattered to him was the journey. He would never reach his ultimate destination, of this I was certain.

"I see I have somewhat overwhelmed you," Moreau said, his face kindly, like that of a reassuring uncle. "Fear not. As we continue our journey, you will learn. Why not take the rest of the day to ponder what I have told you? Perhaps a trip to the zoo would prove beneficial."

Never was the bright light of day more welcome to me than at the moment I left Moreau, my mind awhirl. This incident, Watson, the moment I knew Moreau had to be stopped, showed me the true face of evil. I have been resolute in combating it ever since.

Simply going to Pike would not be enough. I had observed Moreau closely enough to know he would lock me out of the building and post a guard if necessary should he decide I wasn't to be trusted. Reporting him to the University would have been pointless, given his wealth and power. No, Watson, I would have to build a case against Moreau. This would be the first time I would put my peculiar abilities to better use than scientific experimentation and impressing my friends.

Thus, I did nothing for the next two weeks, slowly gaining Moreau's deeper trust. He finally allowed me to assist him in the private laboratory, where I saw his gruesome methods at first hand. I had to summon every ounce of will to keep my face impassive as he tortured those animals, forced myself to deafen my ears as they screeched and cried in their agony, and keep my growing horror and disgust to myself as I saw them transmuted into ungodly creatures Nature never intended to exist.

Yet, despite my revulsion, I have to say he would have made the most remarkable of surgeons had he so chosen. Heartless Moreau may have been, but for him to be able to perform those delicate operations on animals screaming and thrashing with excruciation, literally fighting for their lives, was nothing short of the miraculous.

Moreau wanted to teach me his techniques, but I simply could not bring myself to do it. I dropped the scalpel after my first incision (and the resulting howl of torment from the poor animal), and refused to take it up again, dismiss me though he might. Instead, he just smiled, shrugged, and had me do the chemical work instead.

As a biochemist, Moreau had no peer. To this day, I cannot understand how he was able to stop a body's natural rejection of unnatural grafts and transplants. He had devised his own centrifuge, an elegant device which separated chemicals into their basic components, from which Moreau was able to recombine them in such a manner as to be compatible with his intentions. From there, he came up with the chemicals he needed for his elaborate vivisections. Again, I could not control my admiration for such a work of genius.

If only he had chosen an ethical and humane path, Watson. Had he devoted his genius to the service of mankind, the name of Alexandre Moreau might likely have been revered to the end of time. Instead, if somewhere there is a hall of villainy, Moreau may have an entire wing dedicated to his legacy.

As Pike requested, I kept a detailed journal of everything we did, and sometimes to this day I curse myself for not acting sooner, but I do not believe I could. Few men are as diabolical, cautious, or better prepared than Dr. Moreau. Indeed, I wanted to give the experience more time, and would have done, except for one animal, one Moreau kept only to himself.

"Please don't take this amiss, Mr. Holmes. While you are coming along quite nicely and appear to have understood what I have told you, there are some experiments for which you simply are not ready. One such is behind that door."

A door with a solid Chubb lock in place, which led me to some experiments of my own in my rooms. I purchased several Chubbs, and spent my evenings disassembling them, determining how the mechanism worked, and also devising a way to pick the lock without leaving the telltale scratches which give every thief away.

At last, I went to Pike.

"If what you say is true," he said as we shared beer and sandwiches, "then the University has embraced a madman the equal of Victor Frankenstein. We'll need more than your word, Holmes. We'll need to get a camera in there."

"Moreau would never allow it."

"Moreau need not know about it."

The Friday next, I casually unlatched a window facing a small wood in the rear of the laboratory, where Moreau and I would refresh ourselves on those occasions when an experiment became a bit too malodorous. The location afforded a small modicum of privacy and stealth. Our plan: slip into the laboratory on a Sunday evening, when not a soul would see us, take as many pictures as we could, and slip out. After that, I could tender my resignation to Dr. Moreau and begin to clear my conscience.

The bright half-moon in the summer sky seemed to smile down on us as we lugged the heavy photographic apparatus through the window and into the laboratory.

"Couldn't you get something smaller?" I asked as we set up a large studio portrait camera in front of a row of cages. We had to set the bulky contraption on a tripod, and of course there was the flash apparatus. We tried our best not to disturb the animals, because if they moved their images would blur. We did not light the room in order to preserve the photographic plates, which Pike immediately secreted in a leather pouch he had brought. We took about ten photographs, as I recall.

"What's in there?" asked Pike, indicating the door concealing the one experiment I had been denied.

"I'd like to know myself," I said, as I set to work on the lock.

To this day, I don't know quite what to call the thing which sprang at us from behind the door, but it had grey fur, sharp white teeth, blazing red eyes, and curved razors for claws, the latter of which sank right into my thigh, causing me to howl and awaken the other animals, which spread the din. Their natural instinct would be to flee, which they couldn't do.

"Pike!" I cried. "Run!"

I need not have warned him: the man's speed put the great racehorse Eclipse to shame. At least he had the good sense to take care with the photographic plates, but that left me alone with a vicious creature the size of a St. Bernard and with the speed of a jungle cat. The thing's claws scored my leg again as, near panic, I finally gripped a wooden desk chair and thrust it at the beast, a round silhouette with red eyes and thin, sharp teeth which glistened in the moonlight.

My blood ran warm and dark as feeling deserted my right leg. Movement, essential to my survival, became more and more difficult, and I do not know how I managed to stay on my feet. The creature had managed to rob me of a young man's natural agility, and it now had a trail of fresh blood. My only hope of survival lay in getting out of there.

In my fear, I had gotten myself far from the window from which I had entered the laboratory, and the creature had me in a corner. As it prepared to spring, I brought the chair down hard on its head, eliciting a horrid screech of pain, and making it angrier than ever. During our struggle, I managed to trap its head in the chair's legs, and, as it thrashed about trying to rid itself of its impediment, I managed to make it over to the window and crawl out, the night air as cool and inviting as a Swiss lake on a hot summer's day.

The most welcome sight of Pike, in the company of a bobby, greeted me as I lay panting on the ground.

"How did this happen, sir?" the policeman asked.

"Some sort of creature is loose in the lab," I said. "It's large and dangerous. You'll need to kill it before it gets out."

There followed a sight none of us would soon forget. Following my bloody trail, the creature had found our window and squeezed through it. There could be no doubt about the thing's origins: only from the scalpel of Dr. Alexandre Moreau could such a thing have come to be. Moreau seemed to have combined a rat and a wolf, a hideous thing which sat on its haunches as it sniffed the night air for the presence of danger, and setting its beady red eyes right at us, as if deciding. But deciding what? Whether to attack? Or how?

"In the Mother's holy name," the bobby whispered.

"There is nothing holy about that creature," Pike said.

The creature glared at us one more time, dropped to its

clawed feet and took off toward the woods.

"We need to get this man to a hospital," the bobby said, lifting me by the armpits.

I could not argue.

The creature's attacks had rendered my right leg all but useless, and I was forced to follow the sequel from my hospital bed. Reports of a mysterious creature making random attacks on people and animals filled the popular press, and Pike's account, featured in a pamphlet titled, "The Moreau Horrors," caused a great sensation. Our photographs circulated widely, and mobs showed up at the University to demand Moreau's head.

"No one came to you, Holmes?"

Pike has enough integrity to protect his sources, so the general public had no idea of my involvement. Even though Moreau managed to elude capture, there was no doubt in his mind about my betrayal. Betrayal, Watson. Nothing less than that. In his cunning, Moreau knew I would pick that lock.

When I was well enough to get about using a cane, the hospital let me go, and I returned to the rooming house, where I hoped to continue my convalescence and perhaps find other employment. The building appeared to be deserted once I arrived. Even the landlady seemed to have abandoned the place.

"Mrs. Powell?" I called. "Where is everyone?"

I received no answer. Looking about, I saw signs of a sudden exit: a table still set, my fellow lodgers' personal items abandoned in the parlor, uncollected post on the foyer floor. Using my cane as a probe as well as support, I gingerly explored the ground floor, finding signs of fear and even panic, but no violence.

I climbed the thirteen steps to the first floor, where we kept our rooms.

Most of the doors were closed; those which were open

showed signs of hasty retreat. I could see where two of my fellows crammed clothes into a valise and exited through an open window, I could see where someone had barricaded himself in the bathroom, leaving in apparent safety later. My own room had been ransacked, but, so far as I could tell, nothing taken.

That left the closed and locked door of a student named Harris. My newly found knowledge of locks enabled me to enter Harris' room immediately, where a ghastly sight assaulted my eyes.

A horrific stench drove me back from the doorway, the first time I had ever smelt a decomposing corpse. The poor man lay on the floor face down in a thick pool of black and dry blood, his body covered by flies and similarly evil insects, his flesh rent to shreds by sharp claws. Down the stairs I went, in search of assistance, even as I choked back my rising gorge.

What could have committed this horrible atrocity? And where was the evil Moreau, the only one in command of such creatures?

After police removed Harris' body, I forced myself into the room, looking closely at the scene before me. For the first time, I used my magnifying glass to study telltale bits of evidence. Paw prints in the blood, for instance, led me to posit the same creature which had attacked me; I was able to calculate its size from the size of the prints and their spacing, a trick I had long ago mastered. Someone had obviously let it in through the front door, explaining the chaos on the first floor.

Because it came upstairs, I had the chilling thought that this monstrous wolf-rat had tracked me there, no doubt by my scent. Which, if true, meant: it came to the rooming house specifically to find me.

Would it come back?

Penurious as I was, a hotel was out of the question, and I made a supper of bread and cheese, determining what I ought to do. I retrieved a bottle of whiskey from my room and took it to the parlor, taking draughts straight from the bottle, pondering my next move. The exertions of the day, combined with the soothing properties of the liquor, lulled me into sleep.

Midway through a dream in which I was being pursued by a horde of rats, a noise woke me. Darkness had fallen, but I distinctly heard something moving about in the cellar below. Lighting a lamp, my cane at the ready, I opened the cellar door as slowly and quietly as I could. The hinges, a bit rusty, squeaked as I shone the lantern down the stairs.

"Is anyone there?" I asked.

Nothing.

I should have listened to my instincts and closed the door, but the whiskey had fogged my judgment and I took a few tentative steps downward. Still nothing. Reaching the bottom, I shined the light into every corner I could see. Deciding the noise had been a part of my dream, I decided to hobble back up the stairs and find a policeman.

Sharp claws dug into my ankles as I reached the third step, and I tumbled backwards. With a hiss, the grey-furred creature from the lab, its red eyes blazing with victory, made to leap upon me, but I brought the cane down on its head. The creature ejaculated a sudden and shrill shriek, and I flailed again, striking one of its paws.

"Nelson!" snapped a command. "Heel!"

Alexandre Moreau stepped into the light as the creature meekly took its place at his side.

"I have come to hold you to account, Mr. Sherlock Holmes," he said. "You could have been hailed as one of history's great scientists. Now, only a tombstone will reflect your name for posterity."

"Doctor Moreau, you are a genuine madman!" I cried.

"I don't know how you created these—these—things, but they are unnatural and unholy. I know you will eventually try to modify human beings one day. I will not let them suffer as these animals have."

"Why not? Are not the streets filled with criminals who have earned punishment? We sentence people to hang for the public's entertainment. Do you not consider that barbaric?"

"That is justice, not science."

"They can be the same thing. You think you have stopped me, Sherlock Holmes. I tell you I have just begun."

I made a move toward the stairs, but Moreau gestured and the creature he called "Nelson" bared its sharp, glistening teeth.

"He hasn't been fed in a while," said Moreau.

My mind raced. I fumbled for my cigarettes to calm myself.

"The condemned man's last request," Moreau said.

"Please allow me this one final pleasure," I said.

"Very well. You may finish it in the parlor. I have arranged transport. I am sad to say you will be remembered as nothing more than a sad suicide found floating in the Thames. You had great potential. But a more creative death would arouse suspicion, and I must be on my way."

I hobbled slowly up the steps, my cane a vital support, followed by Nelson, and then Moreau. The cellar door opened into the kitchen; I glanced with some longing at the rear door, but I could not outrun the creature, so I made my way past the oven, which Mrs. Powell fueled with wood lit by newspaper. I dropped my cigarette on top of the pile as I made my way through the dining room into the parlor.

Once settled in our places, I in an armchair and Moreau on the sofa, he said, "And now we wait. I have arranged for transport to come here at eight o'clock."

"Then you can tell me why Harris had to die."

"The young man upstairs?" Moreau shrugged. "He could not escape in time and decided to take a stand. He had a letter opener, and he foolishly nicked Nelson with it. I daresay Harris? Yes? Harris learned a great deal about pain on that occasion."

"You just left him to rot on the floor," I said. "Did you even attempt to tend to his wounds?"

"I could not," Moreau replied. "Too late. Nelson struck deep and severed the common femoral artery in Mr. Harris' right leg. He bled to death quickly."

Nelson suddenly raised his head, his ratlike whiskers twitching.

"What is it?" Moreau asked, swinging his head toward the kitchen.

Smoke began to filter under the door.

"What did you do?" Moreau demanded, rising. "Nelson, stay!"

Moreau went to investigate. As I had hoped, the newspaper caught fire and lit the kindling in the woodbox. Nelson chittered and looked about, uncertain of what to do, but poised for attack. I took the brief opportunity to tear some pages from a magazine and light those, placing them under a wooden end table. By now, Nelson had decided on self-preservation, and his head thrashed to and fro, looking for an egress.

I fashioned a torch from the magazine's remnants, and thrust it at Nelson, which uttered a painful shriek, and jumped away from me. I hobbled over to the window and opened it, allowing fresh air to fuel the growing blaze in the parlor even as I clambered out. Moreau's bursting back into the parlor was, I thought, my last sight of that evil man.

By now, neighbors had seen the smoke and raised the hue and cry. I took advantage of the chaos to make my escape, safe at last from the evil embodied in Dr. Alexandre Moreau.

Challenger's Journal

January, 1887

It is fortunate that sounds carry in the underworld of London, for that is how we followed the thing which gorged on our bait. That is a rat's normal behavior, but something unusual caught my attention, the sound of things hitting the bottom of a bucket. How could that be? Ordinarily, rats will cover up excess food for future consumption and leave it where it is, but collecting food for later use? This phenomenon would represent a long stride in rodent intelligence.

Though we were at some distance, when Jones stared at the creature, disbelief raced across his countenance, his eyes bulging with fear. I saw his hands shaking, and had I not taken his arm, he would have bolted.

"My God, Challenger, what is it?" he whispered. "That's not a rat, is it? It can't be!"

"I don't know. There's nothing quite like this in any literature with which I'm familiar."

"Let's get some policemen. I'm not going after that thing."

"Where's your revolver?"

"I don't have one."

I had anticipated this, and handed him a spare I borrowed from his brother.

"You're the social reformer, correct? You want to purge the vermin? Take the gun."

When the horrid creature left, Jones lit a lantern, the light of which we dimmed with smoked glass so as not to alarm our quarry. Yet it cast enough light so we could follow the rodent's tracks down a slimy, narrow tunnel, where, we saw, those tracks joined with the tracks of others of its kind. I counted at least six.

Down into the depths they went, Jones and I close upon their trail. The narrow tunnels eventually became wider, and we saw, to our amazement, flickering torchlight ahead.

"Challenger!" whispered Jones. "Could these creatures have a master?"

"That would explain a great deal," I hissed back. "But those sounds. It's English. They're talking!"

We heard the sort of chatter not unlike that before an anticipated event, the sounds of people making conversation before the formal commencement. When we rounded a corner, the most amazing sight greeted our eyes. Majestic Roman arches looked out upon a strange gathering, the atmosphere fraught with portent as something, clearly, had been planned.

"What could this be?" Jones wondered.

"It looks like an ancient Roman temple, or rather, what's left of it," I told him. "I wonder who else knows about it?"

An archeologist would have been in heaven. Somehow, these Rat Men (as subsequent events have forced me to call them) had discovered the ruins of a temple which had to date back to antiquity. I have an indifferent interest in history, so I could not identify the face of the god looking over the congregation. Jones speculated that perhaps early Christians had taken the space over, due to the arrangement of its seating. However, there were none of the usual signs of Christian worship, at least, nothing I recognized as especially Christian. Built of sturdy granite blocks with a great slate stage, it featured a makeshift altar which faced semi-circular rows of stone bench seating. No fewer than two dozen Rat Men sat in these rows, their eyes transfixed upon the stage as one of their number entered from below the stage.

No man living has seen such a strange sight as that of these Rat Men, deep under the streets of London. They stood, if one can call it that, ranging in height from one to four feet when they rose on their hind legs in a grotesque imitation of humanity, but invariably they would collapse onto their front paws, as God had intended.

Jones made no attempt whatsoever to disguise his fear, and he yanked at my sleeve, indicating the way back with an urgent shake of his head.

"Challenger, this is too much! What if they see us? "

"Jones, I should hate to think you'd abandon me now. What would your brother say?"

"Then we ought to slaughter every one of these filthy things before they attack."

The scientist in me would not be denied, so I silenced Jones with a glare, and also drew my revolver. I must admit, however, that Jones did have a point. We were considerably outnumbered, with twelve bullets between us.

I saw, in an evil parody of a church service, a monstrous black Rat Man stand on the altar. For the first time, Jones and I got a solid look at the Rat Men, who managed to retain the repulsive nature of their origins and have somehow stamped a primitive humanity on their otherwise sharp and suspicious rodent faces, round scarlet eyes peering into the darkness, their whiskers twitching as if discerning something new in that miasma of stench. Something new like, perhaps, the scent of a man. Instinctively, we shrank back, barely out of sight.

The Rat Chief stood. He had donned some sort of ceremonial robe, once white, now a subtle charcoal grey. The chittering fell away into a hush of anticipation.

"What is the Law?" asked the Rat Chief.

The congregation answered in a bizarre liturgy:

"Not to go on all-fours; that is the Law. Are we not Men?
"Not to suck up Drink; that is the Law. Are we not Men?
"Not to eat Fish or Flesh; that is the Law. Are we not Men?
"Not to claw the Bark of Trees; that is the Law. Are we not Men?
"Not to chase other Men; that is the Law. Are we not Men?"

Because most were on all fours, despite their struggles to do otherwise, and the chant seemed more by rote, it seemed to be more of a ritual than any sincere desire to obey this Law. Then, the chant changed:

"His is the House of Pain.
"His is the Hand that makes.
"His is the Hand that wounds.
"His is the Hand that heals.
"His is the lightning flash.
"His is the deep, salt sea.
"His are the stars in the sky."

"O Lawgiver," asked one of the congregation, a Rat Man with grey and matted fur, "are we not free from the House of Pain? We are beyond the reach of the Hand that Wounds. Does that not make us Free Men?"

"Yet the stars look down upon us, and the lightning continues to flash," said the Lawgiver. "We need help to understand, and I have found someone who can teach us. Bring forth the Interpreter."

Two of the Rat Men entered from the darkness behind the Lawgiver, a plain woman with greying dark hair walking between them with great and fearful reluctance. She wore the simple black clothes of a missionary, her face made repulsive and pitiful by her terror.

"My Lord!" Jones whispered, barely able to contain

himself. "That's Sister Hastings! The missionary who's gone missing!"

I silenced him, my own fascination growing. What could be responsible for this bizarre branch of the evolutionary tree? How could these creatures be natural? How could they believe in God?

"This is the female of their kind," said the Lawgiver. "She speaks of the Law to her kind."

"Please!" she cried. "Let me go! I'm not what you think I am! I only seek to spread the Gospel of our Lord Jesus Christ. Lord, hear my prayer now!"

"Can she summon the Hand that wounds?" asked one congregant.

"She tells her followers of a Great Power called God," said the Lawgiver. "He created the stars in the sky, and throws the bolts of lightning which give power to the House of Pain. God created the deep salt sea."

"Please! I don't know what you're talking about!" she cried.

"We are not of this world," said the Lawgiver. "We have escaped our Creator. But this world is a dark and confusing place. We must understand to find our place in it."

"You have no place!" the woman cried. "You are abominations! You are not God's creatures! You bear the vile stamp of the vivisectionist! You are something foul and profane! I can't help you!"

"If you don't help us, Interpreter, who will?" asked the Lawgiver. "We know not the word 'abomination.' We do know our Creator. Is he not God?"

"His name is Satan!" the woman cried, her entire body shaking with terror, her eyes wide and unnatural. "God would not tolerate the likes of you!"

"God rejects his creations?"

"Your Creator is not God," the woman said, "but

God created him."

The entire congregation broke out in hideous, frightening twitters as the Rat Men tried to digest this intelligence.

"Then who is our Creator?" asked the Lawgiver.

"Satan! The very devil himself!"

"Lawgiver, she speaks in riddles," said one of the Rat Men. "We do not understand. Are we not Men?"

"Never!" she spat.

By now, I had seen enough. I leveled my revolver, determined to bring one of these creatures to a laboratory to learn exactly what was going on. But the entire congregation of Rat Men snapped their attention in my direction as I tried to quietly cock the pistol.

"It is a Man!"

I fired at the Rat Man closest to me, striking it in the shoulder and releasing a spine-shivering shriek I shall never forget. The Rat Man dropped to his front paws, but it did not fall. Many of the others scattered, while the woman was hustled away into the darkness. Four of the others, angry and confused, turned their attention to me. I fired again, but the bullet went wild, ricocheted into the darkness, and struck something which released a harsh cry of pain.

Jones bolted down the nearest tunnel.

One of the Rat Men jumped toward me, but God gave my legs new strength as I leapt aside in time. Running blindly into the Stygian underground darkness, I slipped on some wet slime and pitched forward, catching myself on my hands as cool air struck a now exposed leg, the result of cloth ripped from it. I stopped along enough to fire again, clipping one of my pursuers in the haunch. Mewling in pain, it collapsed onto the ground, slowing the others down.

Into the darkness I continued, until the corridor split into two directions. The Rat Men continued scuttling behind me, so I fired a bullet down the new corridor, hoping the echo would draw them away from me. Fortune favored the foolish; the Rat Men scurried right by the alcove where I pressed my body and held my breath, and raced down the wrong trail.

I had no idea where I was, only that I was cold, and filthy, and badly in need of whiskey. I slowly felt my way along the walls in the dark, my progress slow, time ticking by as slowly as molasses being poured on a frigid day. Alone now, I treated every sound, no matter how small or innocuous, as a harbinger of attack. My mind whirled with visions of what these aberrations, these perversions of science, might do if they caught me. Visions of my flesh being gnawed off while I still breathed added to my terror. Though not much of a religious man, I prayed with all my might that Providence would show me a way out.

When I found rungs in the stone, I climbed them to a heavy manhole cover, which took what seemed like hours to remove in my exhausted state. But, at last, the cursed thing was open enough to let me out into the fresh air, and the welcoming stars in the sky.

Watson's Journal

January 23, 1887

We returned to the theatre, where we were greeted by an anxious Smith.

"I do not approve of your plan, sir," said he.

"Do you, or do you not, wish to rid your establishment of the largest vermin anyone has ever seen?" Holmes replied. "To do that, we need patience, our friend Toby, and a sledgehammer. I will pay for the damages."

"See that you do."

Holmes had formulated a simple plan: put some bait in the dressing room from which the rats gained entry to the theatre, leave a generous amount of creosote by the entry hole, and follow it (or them) with the aid of Toby, Holmes' favorite bloodhound. One of the least appealing creatures in the world to behold, Toby brought to mind a brown and white dust mop on short legs, but his deep, mournful brown eyes and his unusually keen sense of smell made him a prize in the eyes of Sherlock Holmes, who often said the dog was worth more to him than the whole of Scotland Yard.

We entered the theatre at around midnight, by which time, we hoped, the rats had taken the bait. Sure enough, not only was the platter empty, there were also unmistakable tracks right through the creosote. Toby pulled at his lead, impatient to take up the chase.

"Not yet, Toby, not yet," Holmes said in a soothing voice, even as he swung the massive iron mallet at the hole in the wall through which the rats had gained entry. We entered the menacing darkness once there was room, and now we saw Toby in his element, his stump of a tail oscillating rapidly with the joy of the hunt as he pulled the lead and ourselves along with it.

Deeper and deeper below the ground we went; until we were no longer sure we could make our way out without Toby's aid. We passed some astonishing sights along the way; ancient skeletons, lost a long time ago, workmen's tools dating back centuries, and fascinating graffiti, some of which was written in Latin.

"Holmes, we have discovered part of ancient London!"

"Indeed, Watson. When the Romans were here, above us were open fields and gardens along what's now Ermine Street. We know some of the area contained a Roman cemetery, and late in the twelfth century that site became a priory called St. Mary Spital. It was one of the great hospitals of the day, most of which King Henry VIII had flattened in 1539 or '40. Right now, I'm afraid we shall have to leave the discovery of this place's origins for greater archeological minds than your or mine. Come."

At least an hour must have passed before the passages widened enough for us to stand at full height, and broadened to the width of an avenue on the surface. Around us, classic Roman architecture, majestic arches, and what looked to be the stalls of merchants.

"Watson, this is incredible," Holmes said. "An archeologist would swoon. We appear to have stumbled upon an undiscovered district of Londinium itself. The original Roman city, now the seat of an even greater empire. One wonders what Caesar would think."

"Holmes, there's light ahead."

We also heard sounds of chanting, unsettling highly pitched voices, yet resonant with solemnity, and notes of fear and wonder as well. There was something musical about the chanting, as though some sort of liturgical ritual was taking place. As we drew closer, we could see the remains of what looked like a small, crude amphitheatre, in what had once been a pagan temple in the time of the ancient Romans. It seated the most terrifying of audiences: a horde of huge, chanting rats with some human-like features, their beady demonic eyes fixed upon a stage, where two of the things held a terrified woman wearing a plain black dress.

"Sister Hastings, I presume," said Holmes.

Toby whimpered with primal fear, and shied away from the assembly ahead. Several of the rat people glanced in our direction, but we were well hidden in the cool and dark stone corridors.

How badly I wanted my eyes to deceive me, but they did not. These creatures had evolved far beyond their rodent origins. They had human-like aspects to their rat faces, their eyes bright with some sort of intelligence, and many strove to stand on their hind feet, in the style of men. They appeared under the thrall of a huge black rat, someone they called the Lawgiver.

"Holmes, what are these … things? They have speech! And it's English! They even have law!"

"I can't believe it," Holmes whispered. "He's finally done it."

"Who? Who has done what?"

"Moreau. I had thought him fully eradicated from the planet. I see now that he's a greater menace than ever. Watson, did you remember your Webley?"

"Of course."

"We may need it, though I prefer to liberate the poor woman as quietly as possible."

Now the chanting became quite clear.

"His is the House of Pain.
"His is the Hand that makes.
"His is the Hand that wounds.

"His is the Hand that heals.
"His is the lightning flash.
"His is the deep, salt sea.
"His are the stars in the sky."

I shall not soon forget the look on Holmes' face when he heard the words, "House of Pain." The man I knew to be utterly fearless, as resolute as a boulder, as strong as a horse, actually displayed fear for a moment, and he stifled a cry in his throat. But that passed as quickly as a summer storm, and the steadfast friend I knew and admired returned as though he had never left.

"Holmes, are you all right?"

"A bad memory came back to haunt me," he said. "To the business at hand. We should go backstage and see where the creatures are holding Sister Hastings. Once we know where she is being held, we can free her."

"What about Toby?"

"Keep him calm, and he'll be just fine."

A commotion in the audience caught our attention, and we crept closer, this time having to carry Toby, who buried his head under my arm. The poor animal began to tremble, and I must admit I was not far behind him.

"Lawgiver, she speaks in riddles," said one of the rat people. "We do not understand. Are we not Men?"

"Never!" she spat.

A dozen rat heads swung away from us, looking down the corridor opposite from where we stood.

"It is a Man!" cried one of the rodents.

That's when some idiot in one of the other tunnels fired a shot, striking one of the rat people in the shoulder and releasing a terrible squeal of pain. It dropped to its front paws, while, onstage, Sister Hastings, who began to scream with terror, was whisked away, kicking and struggling for her life, into the darkness. At least four of the vile creatures raced down the corridor from whence the shot had come. Other rat people, each of them on all fours, scurried past us and disappeared, and, following them, a stout man of about four-and-forty bolted towards us.

"You there!" cried Holmes. "Do you know what you have done?"

"Race for your life!" he yelled as he tried to pass us, but Holmes tripped him up and sent him sprawling on his face.

"Imbecile!" snapped Holmes. "You have probably doomed that poor woman!"

The man cursed at us and then demanded, "Who are you? What are you doing here?"

"The woman is a missionary serving the Jews of Spitalfields, and from what I can tell, these rat people have drafted her to interpret religion for them. They aspire to a humanity they can never hope to have. For myself, I am Sherlock Holmes, and this is my friend and colleague, Dr. John Watson. Our companion is named Toby."

By now, our unwanted acquaintance had risen and brushed the dirt from his clothes.

"I know who Sister Hastings is," said he. "My own name is Sixtus Jones. Do you know Mr. Challenger?"

"Who?"

"A scientist. He wanted to capture one of those creatures and study it."

"A scientist? Does he often fire guns in close spaces made of granite? Has he never heard of ricochet? That bullet could have hit anything, including us. Anyway, if he wanted to study one of those beasts, it is unlikely he'll have the chance now. Once discovered, these things won't be back. Come, Watson. We should see if they've left any clues."

"Before you do that," said Jones, "we should all

59

meet with Challenger. He is a zoologist, and could bring some valuable insight into your inquiries."

"And so we shall," said Holmes. "Perhaps we might have luncheon and compare notes. But right now, we have a missing woman to find. You may either join us, or make your way out."

"I'll stay, if it's all the same to you," Jones replied. "You appear to know what you're doing."

"Would that the appearance was the reality," said Holmes, "but we are as blind men lost in a maze. I hope Toby can follow our trail back."

Only now did I notice Jones' wounds. He had been mauled by one of the rat people, and was bleeding profusely from one of his thighs. I could see where a solid chunk of flesh had been ripped away. Only the power of fear enabled the poor man to stand.

"Luncheon will have to wait until we get you to a proper hospital," I said, tearing off one of my sleeves to use as a bandage and tourniquet. "You won't be able to stand up much longer, Jones." I handed Toby's lead to Holmes.

"I must tend to this man," I said. "Jones, do you remember your way back?"

"I think so. Doctor. I need to lie down for a moment."

"Right," said Holmes. "I'll see you in Baker Street later. Toby, come! We may need your nose yet."

I searched the area for something I might use as a splint, but no such luck. Jones would have to hobble to the best of his ability.

"My lantern," he said. "I dropped it in the corridor."

After retrieving said lantern, arms around one another's shoulders, we slowly made our way back. Under ordinary circumstances (and when are circumstances ever ordinary where Sherlock Holmes is involved?), the rats running by our feet would have unsettled me, but compared to what we had just seen, they were almost comforting. After at least two hours, and plenty of rest stops for Jones, we finally saw signs of modern civilization: a utility door to the Underground tunnel. The flat walkway must have felt like a comparative heaven to Jones, who was losing more and more of his stamina by the minute.

"Almost there, Jones! I see a station ahead!"

"Thank God!"

Jones gratefully passed out once I got him to a bench, and, thanks to a nearby policeman, we managed to get him to a hospital before he bled to death. For myself, I badly wanted a bath and a soothing whiskey. This night, I felt I had earned it.

January 26, 1887

The four of us, Holmes, myself, Jones and one G.E. Challenger, met for lunch at one of Holmes's favorite restaurants in the Strand, this one renowned for its excellent ales.

I did not expect anything like this man. For one thing, he is younger, I'd say perhaps four-and-twenty, but no callow youth. Challenger is a great bear of a man, with a beard as dense as Spanish moss, a huge barrel chest, and the thickest arms I have ever seen on someone calling himself an academic. He also had a brash and overconfident demeanor, and I could see that being his friend would never be easy.

"I have heard of you, Mr. Challenger," Holmes said. "I read your paper on the evolution of marsupials in Australia. Most ingenious, if a bit implausible."

"You would have done well at the Royal Society," Challenger said. "Those fools can't see beyond the length of their pointed, upturned noses. They dislike having their beliefs upended by genuine research."

"I take it they rejected your bid for membership."

"I prefer not to discuss the matter," Challenger said, signaling a passing waiter for beer.

As we sipped and perused our menus, Holmes brought Challenger and Jones abreast of the situation.

Holmes said, "I find it most interesting that Moreau has given his creatures laws they must obey to consider themselves men. It tells me he doesn't much care for humanity itself. He believes he can create alternatives to mankind. I wonder if that is what he meant when he referred to a master race."

"So you knew him well?" asked Challenger.

Holmes nodded and lit a cigarette.

"You two have made a fine mess of things for us," Holmes said. "There hasn't been a sign of the rat people since our little adventure, and now Watson and I will have to start over."

Challenger cast Holmes a stern look.

"For all you know, they were going to kill that woman," he snarled. "No decent man would have let that happen."

"No decent man would have let those creatures know they'd been discovered," Holmes replied. "For a zoologist, you don't seem to understand these creatures very well."

"Of course I suppose you do," replied Challenger, with a touch of sarcasm.

"I may have helped create them," said Holmes.

That caught Challenger's attention.

"What?" he ejaculated. "You said you knew Moreau, but you never mentioned anything like that."

"It would take too long to explain in these surroundings." He produced a pamphlet and handed it to Challenger. "Perhaps you have heard of the Moreau Horrors."

Challenger shook his head, but Jones nodded.

"I remember," he said. "The mad vivisectionist, is that right?"

"Indeed. It was I who exposed him. Take a look at those photographs, Challenger. Do you not see the similarities?"

Challenger seemed fascinated.

"May I borrow this?" he asked. "This is science with which I'm unfamiliar. You participated in this, you say?"

"To my eternal shame and regret. You may keep that. I have a number of copies."

"Thank you."

Challenger immediately began to read the pamphlet, taking its information in at a remarkably quick pace, snorting at surprise at some of the photographs.

"This is true?" Challenger asked Holmes.

"I must apologize for the sensational style, but, yes, the report is correct in every detail."

"I must inform you, sir, that you have bungled the greatest of opportunities."

"What?" Holmes put his menu down. "What do you mean?"

"I realize someone like you wouldn't understand this," Challenger said, "but you shut down possibly the greatest scientific mind of the past half century. He might have accomplished great things, and it appears from what you showed us last night that he has. Rats with reason? What else awaits? We must find him, wherever he may be."

"You can't be serious!" Holmes said. "Alexandre Moreau is nothing less than an inhuman fiend, a Frankenstein brought to life. He has no humanity. He ordered one of his atrocious creatures to kill me. Left unchecked, who knows what he might unleash upon the world? Would you really create a world of those rats with Moreau as their ruler? The mind rebels at such a thought."

"It's no surprise to me that you are as short-sighted as those dullards at the Royal Society," Challenger said, anger rising in his eyes. "Could you not see? Moreau may be misguided, but certainly he will find the right path eventually. This man may have found the key to evolution! He could answer the most tantalizing question of all: from whence did men come? Perhaps he could even recreate Cro-Magnon men. What we could learn from a living specimen! Look beyond your magnifying glass, Mr. Holmes."

"Moreau wants but one thing: power," Holmes replied. "He creates servants, and he rules through fear and pain. He has no interest in benefiting his fellow man. He had foregone his research into universal blood transfusion when I first knew him; that only provided the veil for his true interests. Perhaps you have never looked into the eyes of a monster, Challenger, but I have. And now I see the situation is worse than ever. He must be stopped, once and for all. This time I shall not fail."

"Holmes," I said, "perhaps we should consider something you haven't thought of."

"Eh, Watson?"

"We could bring the man to justice, but learn from his notes. Would that not satisfy both of you?"

"A worthy idea, Watson, but you do not know the man as do I. Moreau won't be taken alive, I can promise you."

"But his notes!" Challenger cried. "They could be used for worthy ends! They could lead us to the horizons of science, medical breakthroughs once believed impossible, the very secret of life itself! Who could turn his back on that? With Moreau's knowledge, my place would be secure and undeniable!"

"I knew it!" Holmes snorted. "So all you really want is to bask in glory and gloat over your peers. I believe, sir, that you are the walking definition of hubris. You are no better than Moreau. There is no place for one's self-interest in this situation. The man must be caught and tried—"

"For what?" Challenger asked. "Tormenting animals is no crime, and letting a little pain get in the way of scientific advancement—"

"He is wanted in a case of piracy. Challenger, you must know there are humane ways to conduct such research, and Moreau refuses to use them. Think about those creatures we saw last night. Could they speak like men if Moreau hadn't moved into the final realm of his inquiries? He may have gone so far as to be experimenting on men themselves! If that isn't a crime of some sort, I—"

"The narrower the vision, the greater the outrage," Challenger said, rising. "I can see, as always, I and I alone should investigate these matters. Good day to you, sir!"

With that, Challenger marched off, leaving me aghast. Poor Jones, who remained hidden behind his menu for safety, finally dared peek out.

"Well, there is no need for a single blowhard to ruin an otherwise pleasant repast," Holmes said. "I don't know about you two, but I'm famished."

"Holmes, you don't know what Challenger plans to do."

"But I know what I plan to do. Once we're finished here, I'll head over to Whitehall. There are those in high places who will want to be informed. And I'll need a favor. We have a busy couple of nights ahead of us, Watson. Mr. Jones, I'll also be wanting your help."

"What of Sister Hastings?"

"We'll find her, Watson, don't worry. But now the situation has changed, and monsters have been unleashed upon the world. Indeed, finding Sister Hastings is now paramount, for I may have to leave on a long journey soon."

"Holmes, Sister Hastings could be anywhere by now.

How can you hope—"

"I can because I believe I know where she is, or at least where she is likely to be. Will you be joining me tonight, Watson?"

"I don't think so, Holmes. These past few days have just done me in."

"Very well, then. I'll go fetch Toby and see you later. Mr. Jones? Your leg may be stiffer than Watson's is on occasion, but I daresay your knowledge of the Spitalfields area would prove invaluable. Would you be willing to provide assistance?"

"I can't," Jones said. "Doctor's orders."

"Then consult with me." Holmes produced a street map. "I need to know what you can tell me about these streets, here, here and here."

By the time lunch arrived, I was ravenous, but Holmes barely touched his meal, so keen was he to rescue Sister Hastings and, I assume, begin the hunt for Doctor Alexandre Moreau.

January 28, 1887

Sherlock Holmes is a deep, deep well indeed, and this morning he decided to give me a fuller understanding of the events which have placed us on our current course.

"There is more to the story of Doctor Moreau," Holmes said to me once we had supped. "I had another encounter with him a couple of years after the first."

"What?"

"Our recent adventure has disturbed me greatly," he said. "Moreau may possibly be experimenting on human beings, as I had long feared he would. Bad enough to torment animals, but what he would do to people would be the most barbaric, brutal form of torture. No scientific endeavor can justify that. Indeed, he must be experimenting on people. How else could he have produced such creatures? What can the House of Pain hold these days?"

"What is the House of Pain?"

"You haven't read Pike's pamphlet, I perceive. That is the name he bestowed on Moreau's laboratory when he published 'The Horrors.' Dr. Moreau has apparently appropriated it. Pike always had a gift for the sensational, and it serves him well to this day."

"I can't see why you maintain a friendship with that man. He is the lowest—"

"He is also a relentless investigator when he puts his mind to it. Perhaps I should tell him of the latest developments."

"You have even less of an idea where Moreau might be than you do of Sister Hastings."

"Yes, we'll resolve the latter case tomorrow, unless my surmises are very much mistaken." He paused to light a cigarette, and said, "Have I ever told you the story of the *Matilda Briggs*?"

"Can't say that you have."

"Of course, that was before your time here in Baker Street. She was a ship which went missing about seven years ago. I had just started my practice in Montague Street. Had it not been for that case ..."

A dark cloud of fear crossed Holmes' face, and I could see a horrid memory surface for a brief instant.

"Holmes?"

"Never mind, old fellow. To this day, I cannot reflect on those events without feeling heartache and horror. Again, these events must await publication in the far future, if ever."

"I understand, Holmes. But what could Dr. Moreau possibly have to do with the *Matilda Briggs*?"

In due course, Watson, in due course. Two years went by with no word of Moreau, and so he drifted from my mind as I set about solving a more pressing problem: finding clients for my nascent detective agency. The *Matilda Briggs*, one might say, did at least as much to determine the course of my life as any other case.

I had only recently set up shop at my rooms in Montague Street. While I wished to establish myself in a unique profession, I had no idea how to go about making my name known, relying mostly on friends recommending me to their own friends. Funds were scarce, to say the least, and more than once I pondered packing it in and returning to the study of chemistry.

But I had a relative in the Admiralty, and it was he who brought my name to the attention of Morrison, Morrison, and Dodd, who specialize in analyzing and improving machinery. When I arrived at their offices, Mr. Herman Dodd greeted me. He was the very image of the modern businessman: bald and heavy set, dressed in the latest tweeds, and nursing a chronic case of unease, to judge from the nervous manner with which he continually groomed the large thicket of beard that all but hid his face.

"I am told if anyone can solve this mystery, you are the man," Dodd said on shaking my hand.

"You flatter me," I replied, "but I do have abilities you may find useful. Pray tell me what it is you wish me to do."

"A merchant ship has gone missing."

According to Dodd, the *Matilda Briggs* was en route to Liverpool, having loaded cargo in China and Thailand. She made her last port of call in Port Klang in Malaysia, where she took on a small shipment of Oriental spices. The ship disappeared not long after, gone without a trace.

"We are operating under the assumption that the ship

has sunk," Dodd told me. "A Chinaman, Huan Zhao, has developed what we have been told is a more efficient steam turbine than any in use today. We have been contracted by several manufacturing firms in England to test them. Naturally, we were quite dismayed when the ship disappeared."

"Why try to salvage them?" I asked. "Surely they can't withstand exposure to salt water for a prolonged period of time."

"They were hardly just dropped into an empty crate, Mr. Holmes. The turbines are well insulated, you may be sure. The problem is that there are not many extant as of yet, and Mr. Zhao's company won't replace them unless we pay a fee far higher than the salvage value. Can you find that ship, Mr. Holmes?"

Badly in need of funds as I was, I nodded my head and wondered how in the world I would go about this particular task.

Dodd handed me a file.

"Do you have a free office in which I might peruse these documents? I shall have questions for you."

"Certainly. Would you like some tea while you read?"

"Thank you."

I carefully reviewed the information, of which there was precious little I found useful. Besides the turbines, the ship also had a consignment of assorted dry goods, and a shipment of Oriental foodstuffs and condiments, destined for the palates of exacting gourmets. Of greater interest is what I did not find: any mention of debris floating on the ocean surface, no sailor's body recovered, or any indication the ship had sunk at all.

"It is a far greater likelihood that someone has stolen the ship," I told Dodd. "Why do you believe she was sunk?"

"Buccaneers are a thing of the past, are they not?"

"Not at all, Mr. Dodd, not at all. Shanghai Kelly, late of San Francisco, routinely kidnapped men to serve on ships, not unlike our own press gangs of years past. He was stopped about ten years ago, as was Bully Hayes, the notorious Pacific pirate. Mr. Zhao's competitors may be in possession of your turbines."

"We had not considered that."

"Shall I continue? This could prove to be an expensive undertaking, no matter what you decide."

"I shall consult with the Morrison brothers. We'll let you know."

I had no word from the firm for days, and assumed my role in the case was over, until I received a wire: "Your assistance is required. Please come to MM&D's offices immediately." Ten words precisely, you'll note. These men took every shilling seriously.

On my arrival, I was asked if I would be willing to go to Sumatra to conduct an investigation.

"We've had word that one of the sailors from the *Matilda Briggs* was found in the jungle," Dodd told me. "I'm told he was raving mad and had been mauled by a wild beast, probably a tiger. He died on the way to hospital. This may mean the turbines are somewhere in Sumatra. Can you find them, Mr. Holmes?"

"Certainly," I said.

We negotiated my fee and expenses for about an hour before settling on a considerably lower sum than I wanted, but still more than enough to keep me in my rooms for several months. I sailed for Sumatra on the following morning.

Not being well versed in the nautical sciences, I secured the assistance of Lieutenant William Gleascott, courtesy of my relative at the Admiralty. Recently promoted a grade above midshipman, Gleascott proved to be an eager, ambitious young man, about my age and clearly an attraction for the fairer sex. He had the looks and physique of a blond Greek god, and his uniform fit him like a finely tailored set of gloves.

"I fail to see how I can be of assistance to you," he said. "To be honest, I'd rather be with my mates and of some use to Her Majesty's Navy."

"What you mean is you hope to earn distinction in battle," I said. "You spent years trying to escape virtual servitude on the family farm in Surrey, and found escape in the Navy. You injured your left hand about a week ago while wrestling a clumsy and awkward piece of cargo, and it still hasn't fully healed. That's one reason you're here."

"We only just shook hands," Gleascott said. "How could you know all that?"

"Your speech places you squarely in the southeast part of the county, close to West Sussex," I said. "While most Navy men are fit, you are unusually so, the consequences of hard work in the fields and barns of your home. It also shows in your gait and posture; you are not fully accustomed to walking on a ship in turbulent waters. If the farming life had agreed with you, you would have stayed on the farm. A naval career takes you as far from the place as it is possible to go. Your hand injury is obvious from the way you keep it concealed in your pocket and a slight wince of pain betrayed you when we shook hands."

"How did you know I was loading something into the cargo hold?"

"The rope burns healing on your wrist."

"Remarkable."

"Elementary. I should like you to educate me on the nature of tides, currents, and the art of charting courses. By the time we get to Sumatra, I want to know as much about those waters it is possible to know."

By the time we docked at the port in Sibolga, in the

province of North Sumatra, I had learned so much from Gleascott I might have been a sailor myself. Sibolga is Sumatra's gateway to the Indian Ocean: European, Asian and Oriental traders have used it for centuries. It is also situated at the edge of a thick jungle and sees pouring rain almost every day. Lodging proved to be somewhat primitive by our city standards. We stayed at a moderately filthy hostel used by sailors passing through the port. Gone were Gleascott's uniform and my London tweeds, replaced by light cotton clothing and heavy boots to ward off some of the more exotic and dangerous local fauna.

We met with two representatives of the *Briggs'* owners, the Kent and Palmer Shipping Co. One of them, Mr. Rajiv Khan, hailed from somewhere in India, and his colleague, Mr. Smith Ashton Wallace, had traveled from Hong Kong to meet with us.

"That sailor you found in the jungle, what can you tell me about him and the circumstances of his discovery?"

"His name was Miles Jackson, able seaman," Wallace said. "He was discovered toward the southern end of the island, making his way blindly through the jungle and subsisting mostly on fruit. Starvation and dehydration had taken a toll on his sanity. He kept raving about some place called the House of Pain. He said he'd been taken prisoner, and babbled without end about something he called the giant rat of Sumatra."

That caught my attention.

"Did he describe this beast?"

"Just a huge and apparently dangerous rodent, but it terrified him. He had to be subdued before we could tend to him."

"How did he die?"

"Gangrene. He clearly showed signs of an animal attack, and his leg became infected. Something had shredded

72

the flesh almost to the bone, and we saw the marks left by very sharp teeth. By the time he came to us, it was too late. He wasn't healthy enough to endure surgery, though we did drain his wounds. But his strength failed him in the end. We collected his personal effects for return to his family after burial at sea."

"May I examine the body?"

"I'm afraid it's too late for that, Mr. Holmes."

I hope I successfully concealed my irritation at this news.

"Do you have his personal effects?" I asked.

"I'll have them fetched."

There wasn't much: a watch, a pocket knife, a constable's whistle, and some coins. The watch yielded a great deal of personal information and had been in his family for more than a century. Of more importance to our mission, however, were the grains of sand that had apparently gotten into the mechanism and stopped the watch. I examined it with my glass.

"This sand isn't local," I said. "There are more volcanic elements than found nearby."

"You can tell that?" Khan said.

I shrugged. "I observe, I deduce. You have an active volcano on this island, correct?"

"Mount Kerenci."

"Please find me a topographical map of this island."

Gleascott and I spent the next hour poring over the entire island coast, taking what little we knew of Jackson's whereabouts and finding where tropical undergrowth was thinnest and most easily traversed. In his poor condition, Jackson could not have gone very far, no more than a few miles, depending on when he made his escape.

"Mr. Holmes," Gleascott said, "see this cove here?"

"You're thinking it's large enough to hide a 2,000 ton

cargo ship?"

"Indeed, sir, I do. Take a look. It's surrounded by jungle, the entrance is narrow, but not too narrow, and grounding the ship in the shallows would be child's play for an experienced captain. It's not more than thirty miles or so from where Jackson was found near the coast."

"Then let us hope your surmise is correct. Gentlemen, could you find us some transportation?"

We chartered a steamboat from a Sibolga fishing company, and loaded provisions for several days. Crewed by a captain and mate, with Rajiv Khan representing the company, we set sail for Gleascott's cove.

"I don't like the way that first mate is looking at me," Gleascott told me. "I think he may be a friend of the queen, if you take my meaning."

"There's not a lot we can do about that," I said. "I didn't want to remark on it, but you must have had to defend yourself on more than a few occasions during your naval service."

"What? How can you tell?"

"Your demeanor, Lieutenant. It takes you a while to trust your surroundings. Combine that with your looks, and it doesn't take much imagination to fill in the rest. If it matters, I can assure you that your virtue is entirely safe from me."

"If he makes advances?"

"Throw him over the side and take his place."

"You will not!" barked Khan, who had overheard my remark. "They are the most honest crew on Sumatra, and have served Kent and Palmer very well in the past."

Dropping his voice, Khan added, "They are most devoted to each other. Have no fear, Mr. Gleascott."

As we sailed, I studied the lush green landscape, with its many jungle wonders, yet hiding so much danger: great cats, like tigers and leopards, the rhinoceros with his sharp horn. Majesty, as well, when I spotted a herd of elephants making their way through a clearing. Indeed, I felt an overwhelming temptation to drop our mission and spend a year in that magnificent outdoor laboratory. It did have its drawbacks, especially the insects determined to feed upon our blood and sweat with every opportunity. Thank God Moreau wasn't an entomologist!

On the afternoon of the third day, we decided to put in for a few hours just to feel some land under our legs. Gleascott and I jumped into the water, both to cool ourselves off and scrub the accumulated sweat from our bodies, but that pleasant interlude ended when Khan gave a joyful shout.

"There she is! Intact!" he cried.

So she was. Gleascott had turned out to be wrong, but somehow we managed to blunder into the correct cove. The *Matilda Briggs,* anchored to a sand bar not far from shore, floated peacefully in the cove's still, blue waters.

"The damn map was wrong," Gleascott told me. "Everyone on the island should know about this."

"It's almost 172,000 square miles in area," I said. "I imagine there are still a few surprises left for explorers."

Our initial inspection of the ship took perhaps two hours, as Khan and the first mate went into the cargo hold to take inventory, while Gleascott and I inspected the rest of the ship.

Whatever had happened, happened suddenly. The galley had been abandoned in mid-meal, and the sailors' belongings had been left behind. There had been some fighting, but it was obvious to the dullest of observers that whoever had surprised the sailors had won the skirmish.

Gleascott joined me from the bridge.

"The log's no help," he said. "The last entry registers the weather conditions at around noon. Calm winds, smooth sea, and whales sighted off the port bow."

"So they were attacked in the early afternoon," I said. "But by what, exactly?"

"What do you mean?"

"The floors. They have the sand I would expect to see, but I can't detect the presence of other men than the sailors. Unless we place our beliefs in water sprites or a kraken attack, this is most curious."

"I'll check the bow," Gleascott said.

A few minutes later, Gleascott called, "Mr. Holmes! Come quickly! Bring binoculars!"

Grabbing a pair from the sailors' quarters, I joined Gleascott at the very front of the ship.

"There's a trail," he said. "They've hidden the trailhead, but take a look at those trees. There are distinct gaps forming a line."

I looked through and saw that the sharp-eyed young man was right. I discerned the outlines of a trail where trees had been cut to make room, and, presumably, supply timber for someone. The trail meandered in a northwest direction out of sight in the jungle.

"What now?" Gleascott asked.

"That is up to Mr. Khan," I said.

Khan and the first mate emerged from the cargo hold.

"To my astonishment, the steam turbines have been left completely alone," he said. "I must congratulate you, Mr. Holmes. You have not only assuaged my doubts, you have won a great deal of esteem."

"I thank you, Mr. Khan. For your purposes, it's best you know that all useful supplies and weapons have been taken, but that no damage has been done to this vessel, so far as I can tell."

Gleascott said, "As soon as you get a capable crew in here, all you have to do is lift anchor and a tug can pull you out on the next high tide."

"Excellent!" Khan clapped hands with joy. "I'd say you gentlemen have earned your rum for the day."

"What we'd like to do is explore a trail we spotted from the bow," I said. "There is still a crew missing. I should not rest easy in my mind until we have an answer."

"You are right, of course," Khan said, "but wouldn't it be better to have a proper search party?"

"Yes," I replied, "except for the fact that the jungle growth obscures more clues every day. I'm not proposing a full expedition. I just want to determine which way they might have gone and perhaps find a clue as to their possible fates. A proper search can wait a day or two. We shan't be gone long."

"Very well," Khan said. "Keep in mind I must inform my superiors as soon as possible. If you have not returned within three hours, we shall have to leave, and you'll have to await the search party, which will likely take at least two days to assemble."

"We can come back to the ship," said Gleascott. "Now that it's already been plundered, I don't think we have to worry about unwanted visitors."

Gleascott and I spent a good three-quarters of an hour clearing brush away from the trailhead so that the search party wouldn't have to look very far to find it. The undergrowth told us the trail saw infrequent use, and I found the impression of wheels in one of the muddier sections.

"Mr. Holmes, perhaps we should go back," Gleascott said. "We have a trail, and we can follow it easily. Let's do this properly."

"I agree."

We turned back, but a sudden movement in the bush stopped us. A man cried, "Hey! You there!"

When we looked over, a large catlike creature crouched under a tree leapt, knocking Gleascott to the ground and turning its hot, angry eyes on me. I had a walking stick, and cracked the brute squarely on its wide black nose. It yelped, and Gleascott rolled free.

"Run!" he cried.

Down we ran along the trail, but now several of these strange cats, not quite tigers, not quite leopards, and part something else, gave chase. I tripped on a root and fell to my face. Gleascott had grabbed a hanging vine and hauled himself into a tree. I heard bullets fly, and then a crash to the forest floor.

"Gleascott!" I cried.

Another bullet struck a tree not six inches from my temple, and I raised my hands in surrender as a young man, a student until recently, stepped into view. He wore khakis and a pith helmet. When he stepped from behind a tree, his rifle aimed squarely between my eyes.

"Ares! Hercules!" he barked.

I now saw what made these cats different: somehow, they had been given certain canine qualities, their sense of smell far more keen, and a willingness to be led by men. A closer look revealed that the jungle cat's natural cunning had been replaced by the guard dog's loyalty and obedience, a thought which offered no comfort whatsoever. In appearance, the best comparison I can make would be a combination of panther with Rottweiler.

"You can't leave my friend behind," I said. "Surely one of these beasts can carry him."

"Do you hear him?" my captor said. "The man is dead, and better off for it. If I had any brains, I'd blow yours out right here. You two are alone?"

"Yes."

"Ares and Hercules will escort you. Don't try anything. Between those teeth and claws, you don't stand a chance."

After the first two miles, I was weak with thirst, and

weary with fatigue. My skin crawled with insect bites, and I had thoughts of dying in a raging jungle fever, which would have been preferable to what happened once we reached our destination.

What appeared to be a small military compound had been carved out of the wild jungle. A stockade with a barbed wire perimeter around both the interior wall and the compound's exterior kept the outside world out, and those inside prisoners. Most of the buildings were squat and wooden temporary affairs, with one stark, incongruous contrast: a small and solid manse which must have had several bedrooms. It stood out like a castle in a suburb. Near that, a plain but solidly constructed bunker from which emanated the chemical smells only associated with those of a laboratory. But I also heard something else: the terrible, familiar cries of animals being tortured by Dr. Moreau.

I saw some of the sailors through the barbed wire. I spotted fresh scars on their torsos and resentful fear in their eyes, but no one needed my acumen to see that these wretches had been tormented and spent their days in fear. They had been put to work as carpenters, erecting some kind of outbuilding. But the sight of their suffering slavery alone wasn't what chilled my bones, Watson. They had supervisors I recognized all too well: giant dog-like rats! If work slowed down, or one of the men faltered, the rodents started chittering, and the application of some very sharp teeth solved the problem.

My captor forced me through a simple wooden door rather than announce our presence by entering through the main gate, but if the intent was to keep my presence quiet, it failed. When some of the sailors spotted me, they pleaded with their eyes for me to do something, anything, to take them from this manmade hell on earth.

My captor commanded my beastly guardians to herd

me to an open lean-to on the eastern perimeter, where they had stacked the lumber to keep it out of the rain.

"Keep him here until I get back," he told his beasts.

Grateful to be off my feet at last, I dropped into a corner, out of the oppressive sun. I fell asleep against the wall, dreaming of savage animals chasing me and clawing me. I dreamt of flowing blood. After perhaps two hours, the sound of pouring rain pounding on the lean-to's roof woke me. I cupped my hands and drank as much rainwater as I could. This revived me somewhat, and I was better able to take stock of my situation, the essence of it being that the odds were against me and the situation grim indeed. Once the rainfall ceased, I tried to leave, but the two brutes guarding me prevented that until my captor arrived. I could now see that he was young, blondish and wore a bristled moustache intended to cover disguise a defective upper lip.

"May I have your name, sir? I am Sherlock Holmes."

"Montgomery," he said.

"Take me to Dr. Moreau," I said.

His face paled. "How could you—"

"His handiwork is all around us," I replied. "I see he has moved up from street rodents and house pets."

"No one is supposed to know he is here."

"I know much no one is supposed to know."

"Hercules! Ares! Come!" Montgomery commanded, leveling a revolver's barrel at my chest.

The strange animals did not allow me more than a foot of space as we marched across the compound. The captured sailors lived in makeshift grass huts, while the transmuted rodents seemed to live in large wooden crates with natural bedding. The sailors, I perceived, were erecting a second new building, and had just finished digging a foundation for it.

Montgomery led me to the small mansion, pulled a bell rope outside the mahogany door and waited.

After a short while, the door opened.

"Montgomery, this had better be—My God!" cried Moreau, who had become bloated and fleshier since our last meeting. Fatigue ringed his eyes, and I could see his labors in the House of Pain had cost him a great deal of effort.

"I never thought to look upon your face again, Mr. Holmes. Nelson never recovered from your escape," Moreau growled. "I suppose you'd better come in. You, too, Montgomery. Keep that pistol handy."

Inside was an island of civilization, a bold contrast to the filth and misery outside. Electric ceiling fans rotated lazily above us as Moreau led us into a well-appointed office, complete with gasogene and liquor, paintings of placid countrysides, and the shelves lined with books ranging in subjects from botany to poetry. Moreau sat behind a well-polished desk which had only an inkwell and blotter on its shiny wood surface.

Moreau also had a souvenir in the center of the bookshelf, a souvenir which caused me to shudder, despite myself – a preserved human brain, and preserved fairly recently.

"That, I'm afraid, belonged to an unfortunate who tried to escape from here. Fix yourself something to drink, Holmes," he said. "It will be your last refreshment for quite some time."

"I must ask about Gleascott," I said. "The young man who accompanied me in the forest."

"His body will be retrieved and disposed of," Montgomery said. "The rain prevented us from finding it, but by now I imagine scavengers have found it since and begun their work. He'll wait until morning."

I poured some whiskey from a Waterford crystal decanter on a sideboard, mixing it liberally with water, for I knew not when, or even if, I would next find sustenance.

Besides the decanter, Moreau had all the tools needed for instant entertaining: a silver bowl for caviar, a silver plate for the toast, and flat knives of the sort used for spreading butter. I palmed one and secreted it in my trousers. However, part of Moreau's isolation in Sumatra showed in the implements. Not silver, but ordinary flatware.

"I suppose congratulations of some sort are in order," I said, as Moreau gestured me to take a chair. "Your experiments have greatly advanced."

Moreau nodded and showed his appreciation with a dry smile.

"It's all in the chemicals," he said. "As you know, I break certain chemicals down to their elemental form, and recombine them to make the grafts compatible. I have made particular progress in brain research. The creatures you see outside are far more than one would expect from a casual glance."

"Most would shy away immediately after a casual glance."

Again, the dry smile.

"They can comprehend simple words," he said. "Using dogs, I give them the gift of being able to understand my orders and carry them out. I hope one day to endow them with the power of speech."

"No doubt you are looking with great anticipation toward the day you may wield your scalpel upon some unlucky man."

"I may never have need of that," Moreau said, "though my techniques do hold great promise for mankind. But that is no longer my intent."

"Benefiting mankind should have been your first and only concern."

"But you made sure I could never do that!" Moreau exclaimed. "Your short-sighted understanding of what we were doing and your premature public disclosure closed that door to me forever. You have no one but yourself to blame for this state of affairs, Mr. Sherlock Holmes!"

I did not know how to reply to this outburst. I finally said, "What I have seen here tells me I did the right and Christian thing. You keep your slaves in line by the same methods you use to control your ... beast things. Fear and torture."

"Two of the most effective persuaders mankind has ever known. You must be aware you have cost yourself immortality," Moreau said, lighting a cigar. "However, some good has come from our adventure together. I have managed to create more complex and more intelligent animals, and, once the new laboratory is equipped, I hope to begin research on primates."

"Is that the House of Pain?" I asked.

This caught Moreau by surprise.

"There is no way you could know that name," he said.

"Untrue, obviously, since I know it. Everyone does, actually. It's the name Pike gave your laboratory in the pamphlet."

"Hmmph. So that's where I heard it. I put that sensational publication from my mind years ago. You are a man of many surprises, Mr. Sherlock Holmes. What am I to do with you?"

"We both know perfectly well you have decided upon my murder."

"Not necessarily. You have scientific gifts which might prove useful."

"I will never use my skills to further your research. You must know that."

"Did I say I wanted that? No, no, not at all. Your brain is unique in my experience. It may contain many wonders as my research advances." Moreau turned to Montgomery. "We will need special care with this guest. As it happens, your guess is correct. The House of Pain next door is indeed part of my complex here. And now you will experience it firsthand."

"You must be aware that my employers know I am here," I said. "Your days in this place are numbered."

"That may be. But that number is far higher than yours. I am prepared for the eventuality of discovery. Take him away, Montgomery."

Even today, I can barely recall the memory, Watson. It refuses to come to the surface, refuses to let me fully remember. For Moreau did not want anything from me except my screams of agony. In his demonic researches, he had also created entirely new instruments of torture, the sort of which a monster like Torquemada would only envy.

"You provide an ideal subject," Moreau said during a break. "Notice that I have yet to penetrate your skin. I can bring you to the edge of unconsciousness and back, I can take you to the highest of agonies, and yet leave not a single mark. I thank you for your assistance in refining my techniques."

With that, the torments resumed: vile chemicals inducing pain and hallucinations, giving me visions of demons and hellfire. Moreau plied an instrument which pulled and pinched the skin in such a manner as to give the sensation of piercing by a thousand sharpened needles. My ankles were twisted to the breaking point, and simple taps upon certain pressure points led to explosions of agony.

"Why," I wheezed, "haven't you killed me yet?"

"I need you to persuade my workers not to get any ideas," he said. "You will be displayed to them in the morning, and I want them to hear from your own lips what awaits any mutineers. After that, you'll join the work force. A few more sessions in my little chamber and you'll be docile enough. It's worked on better men than you, I promise."

Only Montgomery's arrival, announcing dinner, ended

that horrific session. I could barely move. Montgomery and another servant hauled me out of the torture chamber and inside Moreau's home.

Dr. Johnson once famously said that the possibility of being hanged concentrates the mind wonderfully. So did the possibility of another session in the House of Pain, or being torn to tiny shreds of bloody meat by Ares and Hercules. Montgomery led me up to the second story to a disused bedroom that had been used mostly for storage. This had been cleaned out, and I was left a cot, blanket, some cheese and water, and a chamber pot.

"Don't get any ideas about the window," Montgomery said as he led me inside. "I will have some guard rats stationed below. They aren't nearly as considerate as Hercules and Ares, who would merely immobilize you. Do you understand?"

"You have made yourself quite clear."

After I had a bit of the cheese and especially the water, I forced myself into a state of calm and assessed the situation with the coldest objectivity I could muster. I toyed with the butter knife I had filched from Moreau's sideboard. A will and a way, Watson, a will and a way.

The window did offer a way out, so I opened it, to see the nasty red eyes of two gigantic rodents glaring back at me, their evil black whiskers glinting in the waning sunlight. Even if I could get to the ground, I would not last three steps before the brutes felled me. I did find a little solace in the fresh air, and tried to see some hope in developing rain clouds.

I checked a closet, and was able to pry loose the wooden bar underneath the shelf. I found no easily exploited flaws with the rest of the room, no boards I could pry up, no weaknesses in the walls, at least none I could use without creating a great deal of noise. As the sun's rays grew longer, they crept up the door, and that's when I realized something:

this being a bedroom, the door's hinges were on the inside.

Using the butter knife, I carefully worked at the screws, the process proving slow, dull, painful and frustrating. Ares and Hercules scratched at the door when they heard the noises I made, but did nothing to attract Montgomery's attention. I had, unfortunately, failed to realize the noises would heighten their interest. But, so long as I was able, I continued.

By the time the light had all but faded altogether, I had one hinge free, and was able to use my sense of touch to remove the screws from the other one. At one point, I heard something outside the door; Montgomery had brought new creatures to guard me, as even such animals as these needed rest and food.

I propped the wooden bar against the door, making it firm so that it would be extremely difficult to open. I moved my cot to the side, and managed a fitful night's sleep. Knowing I had a second appointment at the House of Pain first thing in the morning did nothing to calm my nerves, but did strengthen my resolve.

The early rays of dawn poked into my room, but the noise behind the door snatched me from slumber. First the door handle rattled, and then Montgomery began pounding.

"This is foolish, Holmes!" he yelled. "You can't avoid the inevitable. Resistance is useless."

Montgomery shoved his shoulder against the door, but my barrier held.

"Right, then," he said with a sigh, and I heard him take a few steps back. Calculating quickly, I dislodged the bar. With both my hands, I raised it over my head as I stood to the side a few feet in, the most likely position for attack. The door smacked hard inward, crashing solidly down onto the floor and sending a surprised Montgomery sprawling on his face. I brought the bar down on him hard, breaking at least three ribs and earning a gratifying howl of pain as he writhed in agony on the floor.

Fangs bared and claws out, Ares bounded into the room, but I caught him firmly on a shoulder and sent him slamming against the wall, where he landed on Montgomery's head. Hercules, close behind, managed to get some claws into my ankle, but I thumped him on the nose and sent him scampering down the hallway. Blood began to flow, and the wound to sting, but I simply could not worry about that. I would not have a second chance, and after what I had endured the day before, this pain was nothing more than a bee sting.

I took the nearest stairway and ran down it, brandishing my wooden bar as if it were Spartacus' sword. No sign of anyone. Peering out the window, which faced the main gate, I saw Moreau rounding up his rat creatures and giving them instructions for the day's work. He had prepared for them some sort of artificial sustenance, which they consumed with great gusto.

You have told me, Watson, of some of your battlefield inspirations, those bursts of insight which can only come in trying and emergent times. I had one of those at that moment, prompted by the sound of Montgomery hobbling down the other staircase. I raced to the rear door and stepped outside into the clammy, hot and hazy jungle air.

About thirty yards of open ground lay between me and the three or four grass huts which contained the imprisoned sailors, all guarded by Moreau's canine rats. Behind me, Montgomery had gained the lower floor and had to be looking for me.

I bolted, holding my wooden cudgel as low as I dared, and cracked the first guard rat as hard as I could on the skull, killing it instantly. Banging the door down, I yelled to the others, "Let's get out of here! Are we rats or men? If we must die, let us fight and die like Englishmen!"

Five men poured into the sunlight as what seemed to be a horde of angry guard rats raced toward us. The man nearest me kicked at the hut's wooden door, which buckled immediately and provided instant weapons. Though the horrid beasts swarmed around us, they were much shorter and provided easy targets. In our anger, we barely felt their teeth and their heads broke with sickening, but satisfying crunches, their bloodied bodies shuddering with death throes under the brutal sun.

By now, the other huts burst open, and the sailors followed suit, grabbing anything they could hit with, even as sharp rodent claws rent their flesh, and blood now flowed freely between both man and animal. We managed to club our way free and began to rush at the main gate when a crisp gunshot cut through the air.

Alexandre Moreau fired again, killing one of the sailors, and our escape attempt ended as quickly as it began.

"You are a damned nuisance, Mr. Sherlock Holmes," Moreau snarled. "You've set me back by several weeks at least. I can tolerate this no longer."

A commotion outside the compound caught everyone's attention. Frustrated, Moreau left us in care of the remaining guard rats and went to the main gate, one of his vicious cat-dog creatures trotting at his side. Not a moment later, both he and the cat thing ran toward the main house.

At that, the guard rats raced toward the main gate, where the welcome sight of Her Majesty's Marines made their way through the jungle and closed in on us. We cheered as we heard their axes break the gate, and charged toward them with our own crude weapons, trapping the guard rats between us. A squad dropped on one knee and began firing at the creatures, whose true rat's nature showed as they immediately scattered for any dark space they could find.

The canine cats proved more dangerous. Eight of them

came out of nowhere, felling two of the sailors, and nearly crippling me, but I was able to force it off. Several of the beasts circled the marine troop, snarling and waiting for an excuse to pounce.

But they hadn't counted on the second wave, which stayed in the brush and fired from behind the trees, wounding some of the animals. Three of them ran into the jungle and apparently made their escape. By that point, I was simply exhausted and collapsed onto the ground, bleeding from bites and lacerations, faint with dehydration and lack of nutrition, numb from pain, my energy spent.

I regained my senses back at the main house, where a soldier calling himself Captain Howard said he wanted to talk to me. I demanded water first.

"I'm told you know what this place is," he said.

"It is a pit of evil," I said. "Have you captured Dr. Moreau?"

"Who is that?"

"The master of this hell, and creator of those vile creatures outside."

"Yes, what are they?"

"The product of vivisection gone mad!" I told him. "I won't deny Moreau's genius, but he uses it for the most evil of ends. This whole place needs to be razed to the ground and removed from man's knowledge. Otherwise, dark days lie ahead. Find Montgomery. He knows much more about this place than I."

"There is no one here save yourself and those poor sailors," said Captain Howard. "Most of them seem to be babbling idiots. Their tale makes little sense."

"Give them some time to recover," I said. "They have suffered the torment of the damned. May I ask how you found us?"

"One Lieutenant Gleascott, who accompanied you

here," Howard said. "He had a bullet in him, he'd lost a lot of blood, but he made it back to your vessel and sounded the alarm. You owe him a great deal."

"If you have stopped that monster, so does mankind," I said.

"And that, Watson, is the story of the *Matilda Briggs* and the Giant Rat of Sumatra," Holmes said. "I think you can see why the general public should be kept in the dark about this. Science could go down a dark path indeed if this became generally known."

"What about Challenger?"

"You tell me, Watson. You spent an hour with the man. What did you observe?"

"He's young, brash, ambitious, egotistical, and impatient. He could certainly use a good barber to tame that beard."

"What else?"

"His suit has seen better days, but neat enough. My guess is that he is unmarried."

"Yes, that was obvious. What that overeducated oaf's appearance tells us is that he is richer in vanity than he is in pounds sterling. I spotted plenty of subterranean mud on his boots, an indifferently maintained suit, and a beard that resembles the inside of a horsehair mattress. The man can't afford a clean tie, let alone an expensive, specialized voyage. I don't think he is likely to go anywhere except back to the classroom and those students he clearly despises."

"That won't necessarily stop him from trying to find Moreau. His name happens to be 'Challenger." He may well live up to it."

"What of it? He's no different from any other underappreciated academic blowhard. He'll go back to his studies and, who knows? Perhaps he may one day follow

Moreau's path, but in a different direction. Perhaps Challenger will unlock the secret to universal blood transfusion, and actually justify the opinion he has of himself. For ourselves, we still have a missionary to find."

Challenger's Journal

February, 1887

Loath though I was to do this, and with all the humility I could muster, I reluctantly went to the Royal Society to ask for aid. It took a great deal of effort to force myself to go, given that so few members are willing to even talk to me or shake my hand. Why, I can't imagine. I do have a blunt manner, that is true, but is that any reason for being shunned so completely? How is it my fault that they deliberately blind themselves to the cause of scientific advancement? Surely it is not asking much for them to rise above their petty prejudices and entrenched dogmas to hear what I have to say. Science should not be reduced to rigid doctrine and stagnation.

But I digress. While my manners have made me all but a pariah at the Royal Society, I am not without resources. There are those who can look past a forbidding façade to see the truth beneath, and the great paleontologist Dr. Chester Trevor, to my good fortune, is one of them. Once a target of similar calumny, Trevor is the most open-minded of men, and he granted me an audience. Once comfortably settled, I gave him Langdale Pike's pamphlet, which he greeted with distaste.

"My, this brings back a few memories," the old man said.

Trevor had been a giant in his day, a pioneer of evolutionary biology and a trail blazer in the field of dinosaur research. One of the reasons we have remained on good terms is the treatment his hypothesis received at the hands of his peers about 30 years ago. Trevor believes there are places on this earth where prehistoric creatures still roam. Despite some rather persuasive evidence indicating such a possibility, I must reluctantly admit I did not find enough there to fully support his hypothesis, and I have to say the very idea is utter nonsense. But I'll say this: Trevor stands by his convictions.

"What can you tell me of Alexandre Moreau?" I asked him.

"A deluded madman, but a genius," Trevor said. "We were at university together. Even then, he was a little wild, fascinated with the nervous system and its response to pain. My private belief is that he enjoyed tormenting animals."

"What of these accusations?"

"I believe every word of it," said Trevor. "Everything in this tract is consistent with the Moreau I remember. He always preferred to work in private, and his family had the money to make it possible. Of course, he's probably dead now. He has to be, or we would have heard something."

"We have heard from him. He is still alive and at work."

"What? Challenger, that can't be possible."

"I have seen his creations with my own two eyes, Trevor. His creatures lurk under the streets of London. They have both speech and reason."

"What? Seen them, you say?"

"And heard them speak. They have apparently developed a bizarre religion around Dr. Moreau. Somehow, Moreau has managed to fuse rats and other creatures to create a crude and primitive new breed of … something. I call them Rat Men for the time being. We'll have to capture some in order to make a formal classification, of course. "

"Challenger, do you have proof of this?"

"I can summon three witnesses and take you to their temple."

I recounted the events of the past few days. I still have yet to talk to Sixtus Jones. I hope the terrors of that night haven't put him off. Our best hope of finding Dr. Moreau is to capture one of these things alive and asking it from whence it came. For all we know, Moreau is back in England.

"Remarkable," Trevor said softly once I completed my tale.

"Do you see the potential of this research, Dr. Trevor? Do you see why we must find him and use his work for the good of mankind?"

"I—I—Honestly, I don't know what to think," Trevor said.

"Where might Moreau be found?"

"He likes his privacy, which means he could be anywhere," Trevor said.

"Wherever he is, he needs equipment and supplies," I said.

"True. My guess is he would be somewhere in the Far East."

"Why?"

"Because his family has rubber and trade interests there. That's a large part of the Moreau financial empire. They have a plantation on the island of Sumatra, I believe, and gold mining interests in South America. Those are among the few areas of the world where Moreau could elude British justice should that be necessary."

"The man has committed no crime."

"Oh, that doesn't matter, Challenger," Trevor replied. "The public, if they knew what you told me, would rise as one and demand his head. You have described truly fearsome creatures. What if they breed like rats and not men? They could prove a great threat."

"I had not thought of that. I must find him, Dr. Trevor. The man may be mad, but he has unique knowledge which could be lost forever if Sherlock Holmes has his way."

"Yes, Sherlock Holmes. I have heard of him. Some

94

sort of private policeman, I've been told."

"He calls himself a consulting detective, but in fact he is nothing more than an amateur scientist with enough knowledge to be dangerous, and he has a knack for finding trouble. His own encounters with Moreau have made him a fanatic, and I fear Holmes could set evolution, biology, and zoology back a hundred years if he gets to Moreau first."

Trevor signaled for tea.

"That may not be such a bad thing," he said. "Scientific advances should be made slowly, in the laboratory, with full and proper documentation, and they should be done humanely. The problem with Moreau is his narrow view, and he is a man who does not know what he does not know. That sort of research must be conducted under the most rigorous of protocols, and subject to the scrutiny of qualified peers. It may not matter if you find him, Challenger. The information may be completely useless by our standards."

I pondered this before replying.

"We can work backward from his conclusions and we can reason from his results," I said. "We can replicate his experiments without doing harm. We can study his creatures and perhaps find safer and more ethical ways to the same destination."

"You appear to be as penurious as ever. I don't see how you can afford such an undertaking, especially having no idea where to begin."

"That is an obstacle, true. I thought I might sign on in the merchant marine. My back is as strong as that of any stevedore's."

Trevor laughed.

"I can only imagine how the roughs of the merchant marine will take to your natural charm. You assume much, my friend."

"One must assume much to learn much, Dr. Trevor.

Does anyone else here have any ties to Moreau?"

"I'll ask, but I can't promise anything."

"You have my card," I said. "Please let me know if you hear anything."

Watson's Journal

February 15, 1887

I believe I may safely say that the rat people are no more. Human-like no longer, they have become as they once were before the poor creatures passed through the hands of Alexandre Moreau, except for their unnaturally large size. They are now nothing more (or less) than giant rats. Still dangerous, but mere animals once more. A further blessing: Moreau, wisely, has not given them reproductive capability – yet. We have alerted the proper authorities, who, as I write this, are purging the sewers before these things get into the Underground.

I do not think Hastings will be effusive in his thanks at our finding his sister, for she is in a horrible state. Holding onto life, that is true, and very much in fear. But I shall recount that in due course.

Holmes returned to the temple where we first discovered Sister Hastings, but could find nothing to indicate where the woman was taken or where the rat people might have regrouped. We had come full circle, waiting for someone to spot something, but at least we had a better way of proceeding than before. Mr. Sherman had been kind enough to entrust Toby to our care for the next week, and I must say I have had a bit of sport at Mrs. Hudson's expense. She does not allow dogs in her rooms, and so we have been going to comically extravagant lengths to keep Toby's tenancy a secret. We are thankful he is a quiet guest.

This time, Holmes enlisted Inspector Lestrade at Scotland Yard to report any sightings of large and unusual animals. Yesterday afternoon, he surprised us by dropping in for afternoon tea.

"I was investigating a series of burglaries near here, and thought I'd save myself wiring you."

"Ah, that," said Holmes. "My informants have been keeping me well supplied with current information. You'll find the booty at this address." Holmes scribbled something on a piece of scrap paper. "I have been observing activity in the shops. I believe I know who the guilty parties are."

Lestrade scowled.

"I was already close, thank you," he muttered.

"I'm simply saving you a bit of shoe leather, Inspector. Have you something else for us?"

"As a matter of fact, yes. You wanted to know if there have been any sightings of unusually large, rat-like animals?"

"Yes, standing about four feet on hind legs. Their fur runs from black to brown to grey."

"Then you're in luck. Some panicky women reported just such a creature near London Bridge, on the Southwark side. They said they saw it around twilight."

"Capital, Lestrade, capital. Watson, are you game for rat hunting tonight?"

"I'd prefer dental surgery after the last encounter, but I am your man."

"Excellent! So, Lestrade, what other news is keeping the Yard busy these days?"

Mid-February at sunset is no time to be poking around the banks of the River Thames, even if one is armed and ready. Tonight would be a frosty one, and our very words seemed to take on extra menace, because of the condensation in the air making our breath visible.

"I put some creosote down last night," Holmes said as Toby sniffed for the scent. "If we are fortunate—ah!"

Toby strained on the lead and led us along the bank in a generally easterly direction. We made our way over soft ground and moribund vegetation, until we saw, ahead of us, a large pipe draining water slowly into the river.

"The storm outlet," Holmes said. "That makes sense. Those evil creatures are too large for ordinary rat habitat. But it does raise concerns about Sister Hastings' health. You should have brought your Gladstone."

"I have a field kit," said I, displaying the small tin box, in which I had packed some medical essentials. "It should do, depending on her condition."

"Right. Come along, then. Toby's ready to break free if we don't follow."

Running water does not confound such a wonder as Toby, and he resolutely followed the scent deep into the storm drain, and from there into the dank and slimy underground maze of pipes, corridors, passages, built seemingly without any sense of a plan. Yet the place was warmer than the outside, much like a cave which maintains the same temperature all year round.

Our lanterns showed us old, historic brickwork, plenty of support structure in need of maintenance, and, finally, a wide brick corridor with tracks visible in the muddy dirt.

"Well done, Toby!" Holmes exclaimed, stopping long enough to give our canine friend a liver treat. "Do you hear that, Watson?"

We did, a commotion of some sort, but utterly unlike the last time, with its ritualistic speech and primitive social structure. They sounded more like an angry mob, and I detected nothing human in these sounds. This time, we only heard isolated words and a lot of excited, highly pitched twittering. The nearer we came to the fracas, the louder sounds of fighting became. As we drew closer, Toby began to show signs of fear, but the resolute bloodhound kept to the course, though his stubby tail sagged with reluctance, and he kept glancing back at us, I believe in hopes of turning back.

What we saw will haunt my nightmares forever.

The rats had formed a circle, and in the center two of them, one grey and one black, were battling each other. Both were covered in dark blood and matted fur, and their razor-sharp teeth rent one another's flesh with every attack, releasing fresh and frightening howls of pain. We heard no signs of human-like speech, only the guttural noises one would expect from rodents grown to such unnatural sizes.

"What about Sister Hastings?" I whispered.

"I don't think we should attract their attention right now," Holmes whispered in reply. "They have devolved back into savagery. It appears that Moreau's treatments are not permanent. Their animal nature is winning out."

"I never saw rats entertaining themselves this way," I whispered back. "My God, Holmes! What if humanity's darker impulses have somehow merged with these creatures' naturally dark nature? Don't forget, they eat meat, and they're none too fussy about what kind. These monsters could truly be dangerous!"

The animals cheered like the devils of hell as the grey rat took the upper hand, sinking his teeth into his opponent's neck, and opening up an artery. The air filled with the reek of hot blood as the black rat-creature screamed in its dying agony. It fell forward onto the damp, dirty floor as the grey rat, crazed with bloodlust, attacked again, delivering the final blow and rising up on its hind legs to bask in its victory and the audience's adoration.

"Now's the time, Watson," said Holmes. "Let's see if we can get past these things. Come, Toby, don't be afraid, that's a good boy."

We inched down a side corridor, hoping to find a way back to the main avenue, but we got lost again. Toby wanted to go back to the scent of creosote, but we could not take the risk just yet. Finally, we decided to rest until it felt safe to return.

"This does not inspire my hopes for Sister Hastings," Holmes said. "I would judge from what we just saw that these creatures need Moreau's treatments to retain their intelligence."

"This could be good news, you know," I said. "It might mean they have no use for Sister Hastings. They may have forgotten about her altogether."

"But what a state she must be in!" said Holmes. "She has to be undernourished, badly in need of medical care, frightened. Assuming she is still alive, a result in which my confidence is waning. Come. They must have dispersed by now. Let's see what we can find."

The rats had gone elsewhere, leaving the quivering carcass of the black rat behind. Toby became excited, and pulled us toward the horrid creature. Once we were close enough, I could see it drawing shallow, labored breath, but its wounds were far too deep for there to be any hope of survival, let alone recovery.

"Holmes!" I exclaimed. "It's the Lawgiver!"

The wretched rat managed to lift its head long enough to get a good look, its dull red eyes pleading with us to do something.

"We have lost ... the Law," it wheezed. "We ... are not Men. We have ... failed ..."

"Where is Sister Hastings?" Holmes asked. "The one you call Interpreter! Where can we find her?"

The animal looked down one of the corridors and then fell unconscious.

"We should do the merciful thing," Holmes said. "Devil beast he may have been, but in the end, he did strive to reach the stars."

I drew my Webley and fired a single shot into the Lawgiver's head, the report echoing through the underground corridors like a death knell. The shot hung heavy on my heart; there is no worse feeling for a medical man than having to give up on a patient, however vile that patient may have been. There is no more heartbreaking an experience than battlefield triage, the look of terror and disappointment in a soldier's eyes when one has to shake one's head and move on past to find someone with a fighting chance to live.

We lingered over the creature's body for an instant, lost in our thoughts. At last, Holmes said, "The last thing the Lawgiver did was to glance down that corridor over there. It's now our only lead. Let's see where it goes."

Toby began to relax somewhat the further away we walked from the carcass. Our lanterns showed the same dull sight, endless stone and brick corridors, water from the springs and wells beneath the surface making the air damp and foul, as well as cool. We did see plenty of the gigantic rats' tracks, but nothing which could be construed as human.

"Holmes, this is pointless," I said. "We can't hope to accomplish anything down here. Why don't we go back home and try again tomorrow?"

Holmes shook his head.

"Look at Toby," he said. "He's onto something."

I withdrew my flask.

"Perhaps some fortification if we are to continue," I said.

We each took a long swallow of brandy. I relished the instant sense of warmth the alcohol spread through my body, driving the damp from my bones for a little while.

Toby's tail began to wag, and he pulled us down a smaller tunnel to the side. This tunnel had a low ceiling, forcing us to crouch. We encountered more running water, and then the equivalent of a small stream, no doubt leading to or from a reservoir. It also ran steadily down a slight incline, taking us further and further from our original location.

We heard some activity ahead, and, judging from the sound, we had found another rat creature warren. When my lantern suddenly illuminated the face of one of those creatures, its red eyes suddenly blazing with primitive emotion, we both let a cry out, and I dropped my lantern.

"After him!" cried Holmes.

With Toby at the lead, we ran as fast as we dared, trying in vain to keep up with this devil's spawn, until we came to some sort of chamber where several tunnels met. Five of the rat creatures had made their home there, and none seemed to have any human qualities left. They had assembled bedding for nests, and had taken shiny trinkets they had found, probably from the streets above. We saw the remains of the meals they had cadged from their foraging. They had finally become the much larger versions of their original selves, and I thank God that they stared at us with fear, waiting for somebody to make a move.

Toby began barking, and he lurched forward, tearing his lead from Holmes' hand, scattering the pack, which scuttled into the dank darkness. Toby disappeared down a tunnel.

"Damn and blast!" snarled Holmes, chasing after the hound, with myself bringing up the rear. "Toby! Come here!"

All we heard from the dog was its low, anxious barking up ahead, a bark with a mournful tone in its voice. He had cornered two of the rat things, and they shied back from him, terror in their eyes, and working up the courage to pounce.

"Where is the Interpreter?" Holmes demanded.

In reply, one of the rats launched itself at Holmes, forcing me to shoot it in mid-air. It screamed as the bullet tore into its shoulder, and its companion bolted behind us, out of sight into the darkness. The evil brown monster hissed at us, and I shot it again, silencing its horrid voice forever.

"Thank you, Watson. That was—"

A sound from nearby. It might have been a cough, or a muffled cry, or just an echo.

"Did that sound human?" I asked.

"It didn't sound rattish," Holmes replied. "Let's investigate."

About five minutes later, a sad sight greeted our eyes. We found an emaciated Sister Hastings lying insensible on the cold stone tunnel floor curled into the position of a fetus in the womb to try to preserve warmth. Her skin white as a corpse's, her breathing thin, her body temperature much lower than it should have been.

"We need to get her out of here, Holmes," I said. "She's hypothermic and in shock."

I poured some brandy down her throat, which produced that most welcome sound of a sputtering cough.

"We came here for you, Charlotte," I said as soothingly as I could. "We're taking you to safety."

The poor woman, whose hair had gone as white as her skin, stared at us in mute confusion. But she was too weak to put up any resistance as I hoisted her body over my shoulder the way I had often done with wounded soldiers.

"Any indication as to a way out?" I asked.

Toby was finishing a liver treat as Holmes said, "I believe so. I hear the sounds of water-powered machinery down this tunnel. We may be near a mill. And if we are, then someone has a very bad rat problem, I'll wager."

Before we could find that machinery, I spotted a set of rungs leading upward, to a manhole cover. Holmes went ahead first to open it up and to take Sister Hastings under the arms as we emerged into the cold February night air. I could see we were somewhere in Southwark.

"We can't be far from St. Thomas's," I said. "Fetch a cab or an ambulance, would you, Holmes? Right now, our primary duty is to get this woman out of the cold and warm her up."

It took Holmes several agonizingly long minutes to return with a cab, and Holmes offered to give the cabby a sovereign if we got to the hospital in less than five minutes. During the ride, Holmes and I covered the poor woman with our coats and gave her some more brandy. Her breathing became more regular, an encouraging sign.

"We're nearly there, Charlotte," I whispered into her ear. "You'll be in a safe and warm bed soon."

Her hand lashed out and scored my cheek, tearing a small gash and forcing us to subdue her.

"She doesn't even know we're here," I said. "That was an automatic defensive reaction."

"Poor creature hasn't seen sunshine in weeks," said Holmes. "I can't blame her."

Once we arrived, Holmes dashed inside to fetch orderlies and a stretcher. As they took Sister Hastings inside, I said, "Holmes, you should return to Baker Street. I should give Sister Hastings a thorough and proper examination."

"I agree," he said. "Take as much time as you need, old fellow. Send me a telegram in the morning."

I spent the night at Sister Hastings' side, holding her hand and sleeping fitfully on a lumpy sofa kept nearby for visitors. Her body temperature had fallen to the point where she might have died soon had we not found her. The doctors administered hot compresses, fresh bedclothes, and bed rest under woolen blankets.

Over the night, she gradually started to move, and, from some of her violent movements, her dreams must have been frightening. She kicked her blankets off more than once, and even got out of bed to curl up on the floor. I finally left at around eight o'clock, hoping to get a few winks and a shave before advising my old friend that we had found his sister.

Holmes sent Hastings a telegram to meet later at a restaurant in the Strand.

"Well, Watson, you look quite the mess," said Hastings; it must have been obvious I hadn't slept well. "I haven't seen you that beaten up since Maiwand."

"We have welcome news, Hastings," I said as the waiter poured coffee. "Charlotte is alive and recuperating at St. Thomas's."

Hastings beamed and said, "This is welcome news indeed! Mr. Holmes, Watson, I cannot thank you enough! When can I see her?"

"Speaking as her doctor, I have to advise that you give her some time to recover. She has been through a terrible ordeal; she's lost a great deal of weight, and nearly froze to death. She has not even seen daylight nor drawn a breath of fresh air for nearly a month. And the experience may well have driven her mad. "

"But what happened to her? Where has she been?"

"I am about to tell you a fantastic tale, sir," said Holmes. "You will find it hard to believe, but I assure you ever word I am about to tell you is nothing less than God's honest truth."

So the tale began, and I could see Hastings vacillating between horror and disbelief as we narrated poor Charlotte's tribulations.

"If there is a merciful God, she should have no memory of these past few weeks," I said.

"What do I tell the family?"

Holmes handed Hastings a copy of Pike's pamphlet.

"Your sister fell victim to the devil's work of this man," Holmes said. "He created the creatures responsible for abducting Charlotte, and my next task is to find him and stop his insanity once and for all."

"I'm ... overwhelmed," Hastings said at last. "But, again, I thank you. How can I ever repay you for this?"

"You need not worry about that," said Holmes. "I shall receive my reward once Alexandre Moreau is brought to justice and the world made a safer place. I will begin my researches in the morning."

Challenger's Journal

February, 1887

I began my day in a filthy pension room in the medieval village of Moreau, tucked away a hundred miles or so from Nantes, in the heart of French wine country. As I write this, I have managed to charm my way into the *de facto* capitol of the region, the Moreau family chateau. Claret is readily at hand, I have a cheerful fire, and, should the cards play out in my favor, high hopes of finding the elusive Alexandre Moreau *fils*.

The family home is an ancient abbey, built in the 12th century, a magnificent Romanesque stone structure whose lords were sustained by tenant farmers, and altered over the years to reflect changes in the times, and yet keep a firm grip on the past. An imposing structure of grey granite, it has the arches one would expect, including the shape of the windows, with a pair of round stained-glass windows on the first floor. The arcading continues the theme. Round twin towers several stories high flank the center, which rises above them both, tapering to points above the towers. A long central arcade connects the front building to a similar one at the other end, stretching about a quarter of a mile.

I smacked the huge iron knocker against the heavy oak door and waited for several minutes before trying again. A tall, pale man in stiff formal clothing opened the door.

"May I help you, Monsieur?"

"George Edward Challenger. I'm here to see Alexandre Moreau." I handed him my card.

"I am afraid that is impossible. One does not simply pound on the door to make such a demand. You must make an appointment."

"I have news of his son, and, more to the point, I need to find him."

"His son lives here in the chateau. I'm sure our news of him is more recent than anything you may have."

"Not that son, you pompous twit! His other son. The zoologist. Alexandre."

"Serge, what is it?" came a reedy voice from inside.

"A tramp has come to the door, asking to see your father. He says he has news of your brother."

"Another fraud? Send him away!"

"Wait!" I pushed my way past the stooge in the doorway and marched inside, earning a harsh, haughty glare from both master and servant.

"Now, see here—" sputtered the former.

"I have seen his latest creations, and they talk."

"You must be insane. Serge, eject this man!"

As the butler grabbed my arm and tried to haul me to the door, I stood firm and bellowed, "Dammit, I'm a zoologist myself, and I'm trying to help, you fools! There are people looking for him! I need to find him before they do!"

Henri Moreau, for it could have been no one else, struck me on the jaw, and I returned his salvo in kind, twisting myself free of Serge's grasp and preparing my finest haymaker when a sudden command stopped us all.

"That's enough!" barked a feminine voice, and I had no doubt who she was. She and her son had the same pronounced widow's peak, the same pointed nose and chin, and I daresay had the old woman a thin moustache it might be difficult to tell them apart. She had all the charm and warmth of a stalactite in a damp cave.

"Henri, what is going on?"

"This Neanderthal says he's trying to help Alexandre, Mama."

"I don't see how he can. Alexandre disappeared in

109

Sumatra many years ago."

"Now he is somewhere else, madam," I gasped, even as Henri's fist curled again. "He is still at work. I have seen what he can do, and his handiwork was identified by one of his own laboratory assistants."

The woman's severe face softened, and she said, "I have been mourning him a long time. You must forgive my son. He is sometimes hot-headed, as you Scots would say. Please take a seat in the parlor. Serge will bring you tea."

"Try not to poison it," I said to the butler.

The Moreau family lives in the main front building, while the rest serves as offices for the family's plethora of business interests, as well as administering the estate's agriculture. On the inside, a curious mixture of the quaint and the contemporary, with early Christian art adorning the walls, the polished suits of armor in glass cases one would expect in a structure like this, with a grand fireplace underneath a mural of abbey life when the building served the Cistercians in the 1100s. Yet the furniture had all been purchased in modern times, including the welcome sight of a sideboard with a charming and expensive selection of alcoholic delights.

Eventually, the mother and son returned, looking more like the wealthy aristocrats they were. I forced my anger down and accepted the tea with as much grace as I could muster, it being served in the most delicate porcelain I have ever encountered, and the tea of a variety I had never tasted before.

"My compliments, Madam. I apologize for my behavior, but it is imperative that I talk to your husband." I handed her my card. "George Edward Challenger, at your service."

She extended her right claw for me to shake, and said, "I am Florinda Moreau, Monsieur Challenger. Would you please tell us what you know and what you want from us?"

I spent the next few minutes describing my adventures

under the streets of London, some of which clearly disturbed the old woman and her middle-aged son. I produced the photos I had taken of the rat tracks, against which I had placed my own foot for comparison.

"These creatures, these giant rats, you say had speech?"

"And reason. They kidnapped a missionary because they wanted to know the nature of God. To them, Dr. Moreau is the Creator, and the concepts of theology are simply too advanced for them to grasp."

"When most people speak of such things, they do so with horror and revulsion, but not you," Henri said. "May I ask why?"

"As I told you, I am also a zoologist, and I believe your brother is a giant in our field. His work could have tremendous benefits for mankind, if only the rest of the bourgeois world in which we live would see past its petty prejudices and look at the possibilities. More to the point, now that Alexandre's existence is known, it is a matter of time before these fools find him and stop him. But if I get there in time to warn him, then I might join his quest."

Florinda summoned the manservant Serge and whispered to him.

"Would you see to our guest, Henri? I will be back shortly."

Henri simply stared at me and struggled to find some conversation, while I stared with longing at the bottle of Scotch on the sideboard, having finished my tea.

"You don't have a doctorate," he finally said.

"No. I'm still working on my advanced degree. But I am very much a man of science, like your admirable brother."

"And I suppose you expect us to finance whatever project you have in mind?"

"Ask, yes. Expect, no. I'll find him on my own if I

111

have to."

Henri uttered a snort of contempt.

"You cannot find even a decent tailor," he said. "How can you find someone hidden on an island in the middle of nowhere?"

I could not help smiling.

"When did I say that?"

Henri's face paled.

Before the discussion could go further, Serge entered the parlor and said, "The master wishes to see Monsieur Challenger. Come this way, please."

Accompanied by Henri, up we went, the stairs as broad as a boulevard, the burgundy carpet thick and ornate, with an intricate gold pattern drawing one's eyes downward. By the time we reached the second story, it seemed to me a king lived there, and in a very real sense, one did. The master bedroom, large enough to accommodate a small brigade, looked out over a magnificent view of French countryside, a bright winter pastoral scene. The bed itself, a royal four-poster, dominated one of the walls, and looked out upon that view. Furniture from the time, or in the style, of Louis XVI, took up the rest of the room, and behind the large oak desk, empty save for a blotter, an inkstand, and some papers, sat the senior Alexandre Moreau, a haughty man of eighty. His dress was every bit as elegant and *au courant* as that of his son, but no one could doubt who was in command: Moreau *pere*, an Admiral Nelson of the industrial seas. He did not look up from the papers he was signing as we spoke, as though I was of no more consequence or concern than a fly on the wall, and certainly no reason to upset his precious routines.

I tamped my anger down. I am a large man, I am a loud man, and I am a resolute man. I will not be ignored. Penurious I may be, but I have pride, dignity, and a small but proud record of accomplishments. It takes more than money to make a man.

"You have word of my eldest son, I'm told," he said. "Serge tells me you have encountered his work recently."

"Yes, sir. He has created rodents of unusual size, and endowed them with speech and reason."

The old man dropped his pen and gaped at me. I smiled with the satisfaction.

"Monsieur, my eldest son is dead. He disappeared in Sumatra many years ago."

"He may have disappeared, but there is no doubt these creatures are the result of his work. One of his own laboratory assistants recognized it."

I held my tongue as the old man pondered this information before he said, "Well, man? What is it you want from us?"

"I am convinced that your son is one of the great geniuses of the age," said I. "If he can give rodents speech, if he can make rats think, what are the possibilities? Men could be given the best qualities of our mammalian kin. Imagine the ease with which gorillas could do hard labor, or soldiers with the cunning of the fox. Thinking further, is winged flight beyond possibility? These are avenues begging to be explored, and your son is the man who is already doing it. This knowledge must be harnessed, not left to rot in a godforsaken jungle!"

The old man actually smiled.

"You speak with conviction," he said. "I'm beginning to believe you."

"Can you help me? Do you know where he is?"

Henri Moreau spoke for the first time.

"Papa, don't listen to him. He may well be just a confidence trickster."

"I assure you, my credentials are genuine, and I invite you to investigate. I have registered at a pension in the village.

You may find me there. I will be staying for a few days. There are certain amphibious species unique to this region, and I am taking the opportunity for further study."

"There will be no need for that, Monsieur Challenger. I am unaccustomed to such specimens of humanity such as yourself, and I wish to learn more. Why don't you take a guest room here, and we will discuss this further, at table this evening. Would you be so good as to join us?"

"I would be more than honored, Monsieur Moreau."

"Seven o'clock, then. Serge, see to Monsieur Challenger's arrangements, and settle his bill at the pension, won't you?"

With a nod, he dismissed us. As we left, I filched a Bolivar cigar from the humidor on a stand near the door. I was damned if I was going to leave this place without a proper souvenir.

The Moreau family may have a reputation as rapacious capitalists; however, they do spend their fortunes in elegant style. We sat around an oak table that had to date back to medieval times, to judge from the carvings on the legs. Our chairs were upholstered in fine gold brocade, the table covered with a bright white linen cloth. The silverware proved to be genuine silver, the plates fine porcelain china which could have been refined into something musical, the wine served in Waterford crystal.

More than ever, I was aware of my status as an impecunious student. The settings alone intimidated me, as I am sure was the intent. I am accustomed to simple public house fare, my palate unprepared for the rich pate', the fine wines accompanying each course, an Alpine dish called raclette, (combining potatoes, pickled gherkins and onions, a special sort of cheese, and succulent pressed meat), salmon, duck breast *cassise*, seasonal vegetables from the estate's gardens, and an ambrosial chocolate soufflé´, complemented by a sweet liqueur. The Queen herself could not enjoy a more satisfying repast.

Besides Alexandre Moreau *pere* and Henri, two women joined us: the severe and frosty Florinda, and a comely young woman, Henri's daughter, Sophie. She gave me a pretty, reserved smile, which I tried to return without looking like a Pictish savage, something, no doubt, is what their eyes saw looking at me, dressed as I was in an ill-fitting business suit.

"We are pleased to tell you that Sophie has accepted the hand of the Baron von Edelshausen in marriage," Florinda Moreau told me. "Nuptials will take place in the spring."

"I offer my heartiest congratulations," I said. "I am sure you will be the happiest of brides."

"Thank you, Monsieur Challenger. It is kind of you to say so."

"That is quite the sapphire in your engagement ring."

"Most make that mistake. It is, in fact, a blue diamond, one of only a few known in the world. The Baron is well traveled."

And pretty damn wealthy, I thought. *What a surprise.* This exchange took place with all the cheer to be found in a cold and foggy cemetery on a dark night.

Conversation drifted to other matters. We chatted genially, and carefully, about scientific matters, with Sophie asking me intelligent questions about zoology and botany, the sort of questions which implied education and learning. Imagine! A young woman of her class actually conversant on topics other than herself, her clothes, her friends, and her money.

"Have you studied the biological sciences, *Mademoiselle*? You appear to be better educated than many women of your class, if I may say so."

"Do you consort with many such women, Mr. Challenger?"

I tried not to blush as I replied, "'Consort' is not the word I would use. I have had the honor to educate their sons."

Their bored, uninterested, dense and ignorant sons, I thought, chafing at the endless politeness and superficiality of our conversation. Give me a good, lively Scottish pub any day.

"Alexandre wants the best for all his children," Florinda said. "That includes education."

"Did you learn it here, or at your uncle's knee?" I asked.

I had committed a *faux pas*. I almost melted into my boots; rare is the situation in which I am not at least the intellectual equal of those around me. Even that happens so seldom I never think about it. The fact is I have few genuine peers. I do not consider myself immodest for saying that, because it is the simple fact.

"I apologize," I said to everyone. "I am unaccustomed to your ways."

"Do not trouble, Mr. Challenger," the old man said from his regal throne at the head of the table. "We hear his name so little, and the horrible things we hear about him make him a sensitive topic for discussion."

"He is the reason I am here," I said.

"We will talk about that over brandy and cigars," the old man said. "Women need not be exposed to certain matters, however well-educated they may be."

"What do you know of my uncle?" Sophie asked. "Have you seen him?"

I shook my head, and replied, "I have encountered some of his extraordinary work, and it is imperative that I find him before someone else does. The hourglass is running."

With a simple hand gesture, old Moreau silenced

further conversation immediately. He signaled a servant to lead the women from the room, but Sophie would have none of it.

"I am no serving girl whose ears need protection," she said. "Soon I will be a baroness. It is time I started being treated as such."

"You are young and willful," Florinda told her granddaughter, "and I do not deem you fit for such knowledge. Your uncle has done some abominable things, and he is best left forgotten."

"Please," Henri said, and at that the women rose to go.

"We'd best continue this discussion in the library," the elder Moreau said, rising as the servants began to clear the table.

The Moreau library rivaled those of Britain's great country houses, the shelves rising two stories, most packed with books ancient and modern, the floors thick with lush Oriental carpeting, large portraits of Moreau ancestors staring down at everyone from a great height in their gilded frames. Serge poured brandy from a large decanter on the sideboard, and our modern overstuffed armchairs seemed out of place in such a room.

"I have these imported from Cuba," Moreau said, clipping the end of a long, patrician cigar and handing it to me. "You said earlier that you knew what you had seen was the result of my son's handiwork because a lab assistant recognized it."

I nodded.

"Who was that? Do you remember his name?"

"Sherlock Holmes. These days he calls himself a consulting detective. I understand he mostly works for Scotland Yard. He is certainly no biologist."

"It was he who ruined Alexandre's reputation," said the senior Moreau. "He has proven to be a thorn in our sides

117

on more than one occasion."

"He wants to find your son and stop him, and I know enough of the man to believe he is just the fanatic to do it."

"It was this same Holmes who drove Alexandre into hiding after the affair in Sumatra," Henri said. "And now you tell us he is on the trail again?"

"Yes, that is the case. I must get there first to save Dr. Moreau. The potential benefits to all mankind are simply too great."

"Did you read that libelous scandal sheet?" asked the patriarch.

"I did. It is my belief that an ignorant public can't see past its own provincialism and short-sighted thinking to the true strides Dr. Moreau has made in the interest of science and the betterment of us all. Sherlock Holmes does not see what the visionary scientist sees. He sees only the grotesque. I see the next step in human evolution. I see nothing less than the complete fulfillment of human potential. What true scientist could deny himself that?"

"How do you propose to stop Mr. Holmes?"

"I don't. Your son can work anywhere in the world. I would like simply to rescue him and help him continue his work. Ideally, I would serve as his assistant. I feel there is much I can learn."

"Henri, what do you think?"

Henri sipped copiously before he spoke, enmity radiating from his every pore.

"I believe you are sincere," he said, "and I believe your proposed course of action has the best of intentions. But who are you to undertake such a mission? You are gauche and poor. I am not persuaded you should work for my brother, even if, by some miracle of God, you should even find him."

"Tell me where he is, provide me with a boat and crew, and I can do it. Holmes has no idea whatsoever of Dr.

Moreau's whereabouts."

"What makes you think we know?" asked the old man.

"As I told you before. Dr. Moreau cannot do his work without a specially equipped laboratory, and only you, with your great wealth, can make that possible. No one else could get him the equipment and supplies he needs, and do it in secret. You have to know where he is. Just put me on the next boat. You will have had all the time you need to prepare his next laboratory by the time we return."

Silence descended as father and son pondered my proposal. I did my best not to gulp the exquisite Napoleon brandy, or puff the cigar like a cheap cheroot.

The elder Moreau spoke.

"I have not seen my son in more than ten years, and my time is waning. I should like to speak to him again before I am gone. Will you excuse us while Henri and I discuss this privately? Sophie can show you her greenhouse."

"I would be honored, Monsieur Moreau."

Moreau instructed the servant to find Sophie, whose "greenhouse" turned out to be a vast indoor field of flowers: chrysanthemums, gladiolas, lilies, carnations, fragrant and exotic species completely unknown to me. They were laid out in row after row in rich, well irrigated soil, the temperature kept at a steady 85 degrees, with considerable humidity. I could not control the sweat beading on my brow; the lovely doll at my side scarcely seemed to notice any of it.

"This is your hobby?" I asked, unable to keep the wonder from my voice.

For the first time, Sophie smiled and laughed, the sound like tinkling bells. The fragrance proved a bit intoxicating, though the brandy considerably aided that feeling. I found Sophie's presence intoxicating, and beat down a sudden urge to kiss her.

"I should like to talk with your florist," said I. "I

recognize some sophisticated hybrids here."

"I am my own florist," the girl said with pride. "I instruct the staff on the care and creation of these flowers. They are my passion, my solace. Let me show you something."

Sophie led me to the section where she grew her roses, directing my attention to one bush in particular. The petals alternated in color between red and white in a manner I had never encountered before. The outer row of petals red, the next one in white, and so on, to a white dot at the center.

"It's not quite there yet," Sophie said, the pride evident in her voice. "I want a pink and white variety. That would be more pleasing to the eye, don't you think? I will name it the Moreau Rose, of course."

"It deserves nothing less," I said, with sincere admiration. "Clearly, science runs in your family's veins."

"I was just ten when my uncle left England, and my mother died giving birth to my sister. Except for occasional holidays and my schooling, I know little of life outside these walls. As a girl, I discovered I had a knack for horticulture, and I like to use it to create beauty. I hope to publish my results someday. Cross-breeding and hybridization fascinate me."

"And you have employed that fascination with considerable success. Are they entirely for your family's enjoyment?"

Again, that lilting laugh.

"Grandfather would never allow that," she said. "When the flowers are ready for transplant, we take them to the gardens. We also supply the local florists, and, thanks to refrigerated railroad cars, we can take our flowers all over Europe. The less spectacular varieties are planted on farms around the estate to give them some beauty and to supply the apiaries with pollen for honey. Nothing goes to waste in a

Moreau enterprise."

"Will you have to give this up after your wedding?"

The smile faded.

"You must swear silence," she said, "but I have to tell someone, or I will burst. The Baron is fifty years old and a corpulent drunkard, but he is wealthy enough to satisfy Grandfather that he is not interested in me for my money alone. He is, in fact, the owner of a railroad company. Grandfather wants it, and I am to be the unwilling prize. I was able to get the Baron to agree to let me have my greenhouse, in exchange for proving a male heir."

"Sold in marriage with no more rights than a slave," I grumbled. "Don't you get any money from your flowers?"

"Only what Grandfather allows. Most of it goes to the estate."

I could not restrain a harsh oath, which both shocked and secretly pleased Sophie.

"I am most heartily offended to hear this," I said. "You could be to botany what your uncle could be to zoology."

"Is that why you seek him? What has he done?"

"Now I must ask your silence, or my visit is for naught. Your uncle, Dr. Moreau, has endowed animals with reason and speech."

I had often heard of a jaw dropping, but until that moment I did not know it ever actually happened.

"Surely that is not possible!"

"I have seen the results with my own eyes, and a former laboratory assistant gave me his name. He seeks to stop your uncle. I plan to save him."

"Where is he?"

"I don't know, but someone here does. If I am successful, I'll be on my way soon."

"Then I wish you Godspeed, sir. "

Was there just the hint of reluctance in her voice? My heart leapt at the thought.

"M'selle, must you go through with this cold arrangement? Can't you at least find someone younger and more agreeable?"

Sophie shook her head.

"Grandfather gets his way," she said.

"You have my sympathies. I would help you if I could."

She gave my hand a gentle squeeze.

"I know you would, and I appreciate it," she said.

The servant called my name.

"I am summoned," I said. "May I bid you good night?"

"Good night, Monsieur Challenger."

I had hoped for another of those superb cigars, but no such luck. Henri had left. Moreau, looking drained and irascible, said, "I am quite tired, M'sieu Challenger. Ordinarily, I do not remain up so late, but you have brought to us the most extraordinary proposal, worthy of full consideration. We will need to examine the matter more fully in the morning. I'm sure you understand. I will give you my answer tomorrow."

"I am grateful for your consideration," I said. "I thank you for your excellent repast and bid you a very good night."

"Good night."

I found myself in no condition to sleep. Quite possibly the greatest of scientific adventures tantalizingly within my reach, and warm feelings in my heart when I thought of Sophie, a human rose every bit as lovely and delicate as those she has created in her garden. I could not think about anything because her image filled my mind, her plight pulled at my heart. I wanted to enfold her in my arms, protect her, caress those soft dark French tresses, kiss those succulent lips, and share with her everything filling my heart.

Visions of a fantasy marriage filled my dreams once I finally did fall into slumber. In those dreams, I had found success, and between us, we created such lovely floral hybrids and needed nothing more out of life than one another's company. When the time came to wake, I tried to hold onto it and remember every enchanting detail.

But a decision which could change my very life awaited. Before last night, I all but counted the minutes until I could leave this hidebound ice palace. Now, I dread the thought of leaving and never again seeing the enchanting flower princess named Sophie Moreau.

My stomach clenched and my heart raced a bit as I made my toilet the next morning. To be so close, and yet … I tried to see my proposal from their point of view. To comply with my request, they would have to admit lying to the public for years, and perhaps to violating any number of treaties and laws, and all based on the word of a possible madman so far as they knew. I have no doubt the real reason they asked to have me as a guest and to take all this time deciding is so that they can have me investigated. I shuddered to think what they must have uncovered, even though I gave them permission. I do not know what it is about me people find so offensive, unless it is jealousy over my intellect and my refusing to hide it simply to placate the foolish. My intellectual gifts are a simple fact, and I see no reason not to acknowledge them. It's not my fault lesser minds can't keep up. Unfortunately, human pettiness is a constant fact of my life, and I have to bear the consequences.

I prepared myself for the worst and went downstairs to breakfast, which the elder Moreau insisted be served promptly at eight o'clock. A broad array of choices greeted me – coffee, champagne, fresh fruit, delectable French pastries and cakes. I decided on the safest course, limiting myself to strawberries, coffee, and a chocolate croissant.

I noticed that neither Sophie nor Florinda had joined us. My heart sank; Sophie was likely to be the only ray of joy for this day. Was this a good omen? Or an ill one? I simply did not know. Frenchmen are supposed to be somewhat excitable, but both Henri and Alexandre *pere* remained inscrutable as Chinese priests as we ate.

I composed a farewell speech in my head.

"Another cup of coffee, Monsieur Challenger?"

"Please."

"Perhaps you might prefer champagne," said Henri, "for we have decided to grant your request."

At first, the import of Henri's statement did not sink in, but once it did, my heart leapt in gratitude.

"Monsieur Moreau, I cannot find the words. I am truly most grateful."

"You have also not misrepresented yourself," said the old man. "This is very important. You may be considered a boor by most who know you, but money clearly does not drive your thoughts and actions, and it is the opinion of those who know you that you might well make a true scientist one day. We believe you are worthy of joining Alexandre in his researches, and we will find a new home for him."

"You are the most generous and careful of men," I replied, my heart racing both under the strain of forcing myself to be so polite, and with anticipation. "I shall not disappoint you."

"Do you understand the consequences of this?" asked Henri. "You will be giving up your academic career, and you will disappear from public view for a very long time. Few will know your whereabouts, and it is possible they may think you dead."

124

"All the better when we share our research with the world," said I. "Who would not wish to have his name on the next step in man's evolution? And who knows what fortunes might be made? This could prove your wisest investment, Monsieur Moreau."

A dark pleasure showed in Moreau's smile.

"Henri has made the arrangements," he said. "You will depart from Marseille in six days' time. I suggest you use it to prepare."

I signaled for champagne.

"To the future," I offered, and we all sipped happily.

Has the course of my life just changed?

As I write this, I am feeling a happy glow, for I have spent most of today in the delightful company of Sophie Moreau, with whom I believe I am falling in love. I cannot expel her image from my mind – her dazzling white smile, the laughter which conjures silver bells, her dark, exotic hair and dancing green eyes. Never have I been so besotted.

I have left the Moreau estate in favor of the village hotel, my parents having come through with a bit of money to support my work. I have not told them everything about Dr. Moreau, of course, and I am grateful they seem not to have heard of the man. Or, perhaps the idea of sending me halfway around the world appeals to my father. We never did see eye to eye on much. If he had his way, I'd be spending endless, boring days shuffling money and screening dullards applying for loans.

I dare not dwell on that; thinking of my family always makes me morose.

Once I settled in at the hotel, I went to the bar for a glass or two of good Irish whiskey when a wagon delivering an order of flowers for the hotel arrived, and with them, Sophie.

"Monsieur Challenger!" she cried on spotting me. "I was afraid you'd returned to Scotland!"

"No, I have decided to remain here until the next voyage of the *Meribelle*. I thought I would tour the countryside and catch up on my academic journals."

"The *Meribelle*?"

"The ship taking supplies and equipment to your uncle on his mysterious island in the Pacific Ocean. It leaves from Marseille next week. Until that time, I am at liberty."

"Let me conclude my business here," she said. "Then I will give you the village tour. Shall we meet here in an hour?"

I took advantage of the time to enjoy an honest meal of baguette, soft Brie, and good red French table wine. Once Sophie returned, we strolled the village streets, where she showed me the sites of medieval battles, the public square where witches were burned at the stake, the best views of the snow-covered countryside, still beautiful and serene despite this being the chilly heart of winter.

Without even thinking, Sophie's hand and my own found one another as if that were the most natural thing in the world. I found myself damping down my natural behavior, not wanting to drive her away. We must have spent two hours simply chatting away in the hotel bar.

Free from her family, Sophie relaxed and showed me her true self, her eagerness to learn more of the horticultural arts, her desire to study painting in Paris, and even explore music, that most magical and impenetrable of the arts. (At least to me.)

All day, I have resisted the impulse to sweep her into my arms and kiss her madly, but of course she is still betrothed to someone else.

"Monsieur Challenger—"

"We aren't at your family's table, my dear. Please call me George."

"George, why did you come into my life now, of all times? Why did we not meet before it was too late? There is so much in the world, and I feel as though I'm going to be imprisoned for crimes I never committed."

"Sophie, you don't have to marry that man," I said. "You have free will. Just say the word, and I can—"

"What a pleasant thought, but we barely know one another."

"True. I could never offer you the life of luxury you now enjoy. All I have in its place is my sheer joy at being in your company."

"Still, we have this time together now," she said. "I am grateful for that."

At last, the time came when Sophie had to return to the chateau. A coach bearing the Moreau crest arrived at the hotel to take Sophie home. As we parted, I embraced her with passion, a passion her own embrace returned.

"Come back to see me," I said. "You know where to find me. I can't just let you vanish from my life, not before I absolutely have to."

"Tomorrow, then? I'm heading into Nantes. It is one of the most historic cities in France. Also, I know where the best cafes are."

"Until tomorrow, then."

One more embrace, and, just briefly, our lips brushed together.

"Not in front of the driver," she whispered. "Tomorrow."

"Tomorrow, Sophie."

With that, and a wave of her hand, Sophie Moreau slowly vanished from my view.

How will I make it to the morrow? I don't think I'll be able to sleep tonight. Thank God for wine.

Must all good things come to an end?

Tomorrow, I leave for Marseille and the *Meribelle,* destination unknown but to a select few. And that means I am unlikely to see Sophie ever again.

We have been lovers for the last week, a grand passion fulfilled. Had I the ability, I would write a play; we meet in secret, we take the greatest of care to make sure the liaison never reaches Sophie's family, we make love with fire, and part only at the last possible moment.

Needless to say, I have been begging her to forsake her family's callous treatment in favor of marriage to me. It is the only thing about which we argue.

"You could transform every garden in England," I said. "Together, we can amass a fortune, a fortune none of the others could touch."

"George, please don't ask me again. The deal is done, and my fate is sealed, though I take a certain pleasure in the fact that you, and not the Baron, was the first who took my virtue. That alone may persuade him to end the engagement."

Sophie sighed, and continued,"You can't know the consequences of angering my grandfather. They are deep and far-reaching. He would revenge himself on both of us. I would lose everything. Would you have me if I were not wealthy?"

"What an absurd question! I've been near poverty all my life. Your wealth doesn't enter in to how I feel about you. As for your grandfather, revenge be damned! I've cowed lions with a single hot glare. I've wrestled crocodiles in Egypt. I have even weathered academic politics, the nastiest and pettiest of them all. We can handle one dyspeptic old man."

"Does my happiness matter to you, my love?"

"With all my heart."

"Then let us just have cherished memories of our days together. Perhaps, one day, when the baron tires of me or dies, we may find one another again. Until then, let us just enjoy what we have."

As I write this, Sophie is dressing, and will soon no longer be a part of my life. I cannot put into words the feel of my heart turning slowly into a leaden, unfeeling mass.

When this affair began, I had dreams of glory and, dare I say, immortality, at least in the halls of science. Because of one beguiling young woman, now I could not care less about science, or fame, or accolades. I would trade my entire future for just one more kiss.

March, 1887

Though I still miss Sophie, I must say the bracing breeze of the sea is slowly restoring my spirits, and I find I can once again turn my thoughts to the quest which launched this amazing adventure. A few more days, and I will, at last, meet the great Alexandre Moreau.

Despite the fact that I have no means to communicate with anyone who is not on board, I have still not been told our precise destination, save that it is in the tropical Pacific. I feel this is ridiculous. I would hardly betray the man I wish to be my mentor.

Our vessel, the *Meribelle*, is a 3,000-ton cargo boat, powered by a steam engine with the impressive horsepower of 6,500, and this translates into 18 knots. Despite the mighty engine, however, the ship still has full rigging and sailing capability, in case the engine should fail for some reason, or we get unusually favorable winds. In merchant sailing, speed is everything.

We have a most unusual cargo: it holds what most Moreaus consider to be the basic necessities of life: cases of brandy and fine wine, what must be a ton of cigars, hundreds of gallons of saline, various chemicals used in biological research, and several large, wild animals. They spend their days in morose captivity, mercifully unknowing the role they will soon play in the advancement of mankind's scientific knowledge.

This is the first long voyage I have taken in several years, and I must say that, after a day or two of being tossed about on choppy waters, I have gotten my sea legs, adjusted my digestion to sailors' fare, and am finally comfortable. I have been given a small cabin with a single berth, an ample supply of wine and gin, and plenty to read.

One unexpected bonus is my becoming a junior member of the crew. Contrary to Dr. Trevor's somewhat sarcastic comment on my personal charms, I am far more at home with these rough Frenchmen than I am among their wealthy, and a whole new avenue of learning has opened up to me. I'm learning basic seamanship, the ways of rope, and new uses for my muscles. All of this may be useful one day, when I go further into the field and explore the natural world on my own.

Now that the weather is pleasant and the seas calmer, we are moving along at a good clip, and I am allowing myself to relax and refresh myself in the invigorating sea air, a fitting period of rejuvenation before the labors and triumphs ahead.

It is amazing to me how so much can change over the course of a few hours.

This morning began as did every other; we rise at dawn, breakfast (coffee and sea-biscuits), followed by a spell of work. Despite my recent adventures, I am still a zoologist, and I have taken advantage of my time to catch up on my ornithology. Seabirds are never far from us, and their antics have given me some new insights into these fascinating creatures. I have to wonder if Dr. Moreau has added them to his experiments. Imagine a parrot which could actually talk! Perhaps Moreau has done that in order to have some company.

I have also been fascinated by the sea creatures we have encountered so far. Seabirds are ever hopeful for the occasional scrap, and the ocean's predators are also close by, hoping some of the birds might get careless. If, for some reason, my quest fails (and right now I don't see how it can), then I might make some inquiries into marine biology.

I conducted a small experiment of my own by casting a few chunks of bread into the water. Several of the gulls dove for the treat, ignoring or not seeing the dorsal fin which surfaced almost immediately. As the birds maneuvered so as to get to the bread first, the fin bobbed patiently nearby and disappeared. Just as the first gull snatched a morsel, the water breached and a great grey shark, its terrible jaws wide and powerful, took the gull whole and disappeared under the water. The other birds scattered, but one stayed away only long enough to make another try at the floating bread. This time, when the shark attacked, the gull, prize in its beak, gracefully eluded the gnashing teeth and soared into the bright blue sky, a sign of intelligence. It had learned from its fellow's fate.

A hue and cry among the sailors snapped my attention to stern, where several sailors, some armed with revolvers, dragged a heavy net as quickly as they could.

"What's the trouble?" I asked.

"One of the animals is loose!"

Rushing forward, I spotted a large, orange primate: the orangutan had somehow escaped its cage and made its way to the deck. Our seasoned captain, one Francois Vigneault, ordered his men to circle the beast in the hope of trapping it in a net.

"Kill it if you have to," he said, but I objected.

"He's confused and frightened," I said. "I'm a zoologist. Let me take care of this."

"You have managed such creatures, Challenger?"

"I have studied apes in the field. I know how they behave. Get me some of those apples from the galley."

Our ship had three masts and two smokestacks, and little in the way of climbing opportunities. Two of the sailors sought to distract the beast while two others hoped to drop the net over it. But the orangutan heard his captors positioning themselves, and jumped onto one of the sailors, who flailed helplessly in the creature's grasp.

"Get him off me! Get him off me!" he bellowed in French.

The beast seemed to understand, and threw the helpless sailor aside, over the rail and into the ocean. The others raced to his rescue, leaving only the captain and myself to deal with the now enraged creature. With a seeming snort of contempt, it pushed passed us, and made its way to safety, up in the rigging.

"Well, Challenger?" Vigneault said. "What do we do now, O Master of the Apes?"

"We wait," I said. "He can't stay up there forever."

He could, however, get some no doubt badly needed exercise after having been imprisoned in the dark cargo hold for more than a week. In fact, the great ape put on a considerable show of its acrobatic acumen, its rage and anger fading in favor of joy at being free. It swung from rope to rope along the mast and kept going higher, ever higher, until it reached the flagpole atop the mast and hung there, almost majestic against the bright white sky.

One of the sailors appeared with a sketch pad, and began drawing, capturing the remarkable moment.

"That's Sabourin," Vigneault said. "He's not really a merchant sailor. He has visions of becoming an *artiste*. He studies at an academy in Paris, but he has no genuine experience of life. How could anyone, away from the sea? We are certainly giving him some inspiration now, are we not?"

"I hope he's good," I said, as if I know anything about painting. I prefer a good photograph, myself. A photograph is closer to truth than any drawing, no matter how brilliant the painter may be. I must make a note to ask him for the picture, if he is willing to part with it. It's the only visual record of this incident.

After a while, the orangutan slowed down, and came to rest on one of the spars. Perhaps it was even dozing; it was hard to tell from so far away.

"Time to lay the trap," I said.

We spread the net out on the deck below the brute, and left out a large bowl of water and plenty of fruit, much to the delight of the flies which romantics of the sea never seem to mention in their endless tales of adventure and derring-do. Apes, I don't believe, are particular about their food so long as it is edible.

The day waned, and, on Vigneault's orders, the men stayed below in their quarters. Four of us secreted ourselves in lifeboats, waiting. Not until twilight did the orangutan decide it was safe to descend. Though hungry and tired, it was still suspicious, and did not approach the bait for at least fifteen minutes. Finally, it drank greedily, and that's when we sprung the trap.

The net's corners snapped upward, trapping the beast as we feverishly pulled on the ropes to suspend the creature until we could maneuver it back into its cage. It let out a howl of anger and betrayal, and thrashed about, scattering apples and grapes all around. Lanterns were needed by the time we got the creature's cage on deck, and we lowered the animal gently and carefully, until we could push it inside the door and cut it free of the netting.

The poor creature stared at us through the bars, its eyes sad and seeking pity, not knowing what it had done to deserve a fate like this, its brief exercise in freedom now a frustrating memory. I did feel pity for the brute, knowing the pain it would soon experience. I had to harden my heart and remind myself that the greatest good is always achieved at a high price.

The day's surprises did not end there.

I was relaxing in my cabin after the day's frenetic events, when a new hubbub caught my ear, and two sailors marched someone past my cabin, on their way to the bridge. My heart pounded as I realized what had happened, and I burst onto the deck to follow.

"Wait!" I cried. "Wait! I know her!"

Sophie Moreau pulled herself free and ran to my arms. She was tired, dirty, dressed in peasant clothing, hungry, and cold, but I let the love in my heart warm her, give her safety. I took her into my cabin, telling the sailors, "Please let me deal with this situation. I'll explain later."

Hustling her into my cabin, I gave her a soothing glass of claret and some food. She sat on the edge of my berth, her eyes bright with the nervous energy of fear.

"How did you manage this?" I wanted to know, but Captain Vigneault stormed in, furious.

"Challenger, I'm told you know this stowaway," he said. "This is all we need, a woman on a vessel where the men haven't seen a female face for at least a week! Are you mad?"

"Sophie, this is Captain Vigneault," I began, but she stopped me with a brief and inappropriately coquettish look.

"I am George's wife," she said. "My name is Sophie. I understand this vessel is going to my uncle, Alexandre, whom I have not seen since I was a young girl."

"This is a serious matter," said Vigneault. "We send people to jail for this. Sometimes we put them to hard labor while they're aboard."

Sophie opened a small coin purse and extracted a single coin, tossing it to Vigneault.

"This is 20 francs!" Vigneault said.

"That should cover the expense, no?" she asked, producing another. "And, of course, I appreciate your generosity in allowing me to stay with my husband. Could we have a larger cabin, perhaps?"

"I'll see what I can arrange," said Vigneault, who had calmed considerably. "Please pardon my anger, Madame."

"Of course. Could you leave us, please? George and I have plans to make."

Alone at last, I gave Sophie a proper kiss, and then asked her what had happened.

"Husband?"

Sophie produced two plain wedding bands from her coin purse. Only then did I notice that the blue diamond engagement ring given to her by the Baron von Edelshausen no longer sparkled on her third finger. It must have brought her quite a bit of money.

"I had to guess at your size," she said, handing me my ring. "Now we can voyage together. They will forgive a small deception, yes?"

"Especially for 20 francs in gold. Sophie, why are you here?"

"Once you left, I realized you were right," she said. "I could spend the rest of my days in slavery to my grandfather's avarice, or I could be happy with you, regardless of our fortunes. There is also the mysterious Alexandre, the relation of whom no one speaks. I decided I could not stay away. I left my family a note telling them I have gone to London. They'll scour the city, never knowing what really happened until it's too late."

"Were you planning to spend the entire voyage down

in the cargo hold?"

"If necessary. But then—"

She stopped, and I suddenly knew why.

"You let the orangutan out, didn't you?"

"I didn't intend to," she said. "The poor thing is only fed twice a day, and its cage cleaned only once. All those animals, the chimpanzee, the leopard, the wolf, suffer in the dark, and it tears my heart to think of these innocent creatures terrified in the name of science. I'm sure Uncle treats them humanely in his experiments, but even so, my heart goes out to them."

I kept silent on this. In fact, I do hope to persuade Moreau to forego any studies in pain he might be making. Surely he has learned enough by now.

"All I wanted to do was give it some more food," she said.

"You couldn't slide it through the bars?"

"I wasn't thinking. I thought it might want company, so I entered the cage."

"Sophie! That was an enormously stupid thing to do!"

"You don't understand," she said. "That ape was my only companion down there. I had no one to talk to, and little to occupy my time. So we formed a kind of bond. He trusted me when I gave him food and water, and I began to trust him. I think I took the poor creature too deep into my heart. I felt sorry for him."

"Well, you know better now, and you're where you belong," I said. "I'll keep you safe, my love."

With that, we kissed and retired to my cabin to make up for lost time.

Watson's Journal

March 9, 1887

"There it is, Watson. The island of Dr. Moreau."

At long last. I have been wanting to get my legs onto dry land. The gentlemen at Morrison, Morrison & Dodd have secured us berths aboard the American cargo steamer *Mississippi Delta*, bound for San Francisco by way of Hawaii. Our errand will cost them a day or two, but delays are hardly unusual in shipping circles.

Ahead of us lay a large island with a small mountain towering above the lush green vegetation and tropical trees. For some reason, it had never shown up on any charts known to our captain, one Bernard Morris. The midmorning sun bore down on us, the humidity oppressive, and the wind little more than a warm and clammy breeze which did nothing to cool us. As we steamed closer to the island, I became aware that something was terribly wrong. A thick, black cloud of smoke hung over the boathouse and pier like a funeral pall, clearly the result of some sort of conflagration.

"Watson, the glasses!" Holmes barked, grabbing the binoculars from my grasp and training them on a spot in the water. A moment later, he frowned and said, "I see bodies floating ahead. Better alert the captain that we may need to take survivors aboard."

I took a look for myself; at this distance, all I could make out were bobbing corpses, and I doubted there would be a heartbeat among them.

Captain Morris launched us and some of his men in a pair of dinghies, and we rowed toward the floating masses as quickly as we could. Coming closer to the island, there was now no doubt: there had been a great fire of some sort, and it still burned, though the flames seemed to be diminishing.

The sailors pulled the body of a blond man dressed in khakis into our boat. Holmes uttered a cry of surprise.

"It's Montgomery!" he said. "If he's dead, what has happened to Dr. Moreau? We need to get to the island immediately!"

"What's to be done with this man, sir?" asked one of the sailors.

"Toss him back," said Holmes, his voice cold. "This man does not deserve a decent Christian burial."

"And those, sir?" asked the sailor, pointing to a pair of black, fur-covered forms bobbing a few yards away.

"Bring them aboard. I want to take a closer look."

My poor powers of description do not allow me to accurately convey the disgust and pity that rose in my throat at the sight of these inhuman aberrations. The giant rats were bad enough. But these? They were not beasts, they were not men. They had human-like facial features, but, like the animals they had been originally, wore no clothing. What they had been before they came under Dr. Moreau's knife, I simply could not tell. One might have been a bear once; another may have been a jungle animal of some sort.

The sailors, a superstitious lot to begin with, shied away from the unnatural atrocities.

"Mr. Holmes, what sort of devil creatures are these?" asked the coxswain. "They must have come from the very pits of Hell."

"You're more right than you know," Holmes said. "These pitiful beasts have been through hells of their own to have turned out like this."

Holmes gave the bodies as careful an examination as he could, given the circumstances. Once or twice, I heard him whistle with a reluctant admiration.

"Watson, take a look," Holmes said. "Note the precise

patterns where Moreau stitched. If I thought he was a brilliant surgeon before, I can only say he has exceeded his powers tenfold. He has to be using extremely specialized and delicate instruments to achieve results like this."

I examined Moreau's handiwork, and I must admit the man's sheer genius for surgical technique. Grafts such as these simply are not possible by any medical science I understand; it is as if Moreau went so far as to somehow fuse individual cells.

"I did not think it possible, but he has gone far beyond his early work," said Holmes. "I believe he may well have knocked on the door of evolution. These combinations simply should not be possible. It can only mean he has achieved biochemical perfection of a sort."

"What could make such a man turn so wrong?" I asked. "He could have been the greatest surgeon of his time."

Holmes shrugged.

"Sir, we have company!" cried a sailor from the other boat.

As of from nowhere, a cargo vessel similar to our own had appeared, about a nautical mile behind the *Mississippi Delta.*

"That has to be the *Meribelle*, out of Marseille," Holmes said. "I had hoped to beat her by a day. Coxswain, is there any way we can get to the island first?"

"Only if we return to the ship right now," came the reply.

"Right. Toss these accursed things overboard and get us back."

As we rowed, I asked Holmes, "How do you know this is the ship?"

"Beyond the simple fact that it is here? I sent telegrams to shipping companies asking which would be carrying the supplies Moreau needs to conduct his experiments. Once I found a ship carrying exotic animals, saline, and specialized medical equipment, I knew we had our quarry."

Returning to the *Delta* took longer than Holmes wanted, and the *Meribelle* came up fast, almost overtaking us. Captain Morris ordered full steam, and the *Delta* sped ahead. Over on the other ship, I saw someone waving at us like a man gone berserk, anger and fury evident on his heavily bearded face. Smiling, I waved a rude hand gesture at him and called Holmes over.

"Holmes, you're not going to believe this," I said, handing him the binoculars.

"I should have known," said Holmes. "I'll say this for Challenger, he's one determined man. Can you make out what he's saying?"

"Nothing complimentary, I fancy."

The *Meribelle* lurched forward with a sudden burst of speed, and we were now in a race for the harbor, which had a loading dock and boathouse, the latter of which had caught fire and burned bright against the hazy sky. Captain Morris gained us some distance by feinting toward our rivals, forcing them to swing widely to avert a collision, even as Morris deftly swung our ship back.

"Couldn't stop myself, Mr. Holmes," he said, a wicked grin lighting up his grizzled and leathery face, the face of a man who lived for the sea. "I never can resist riling the frogs."

"Well done, Captain," Holmes said. "They'd welcome you in our navy."

Despite Captain Morris's maneuver, we still only beat the *Meribelle* by a few knots, having to greatly slow our speed to avoid crashing into the loading dock, which, happily, seemed too wet to catch the blaze from the boathouse nearby. Holmes and I drafted some sailors to take dinghies to shore as the *Delta* prepared to dock.

"We need to move fast," said Holmes. "We'll have to split up. Coxswain, please take three men and see what's happening on the beaches. The rest of you, let's investigate that fire."

Following the columns of smoke, we came upon the smoldering remains of a small compound with several buildings, but nothing so luxurious as those quarters Holmes had described from his encounter with Moreau in Sumatra. A few small fires still burned in the debris.

"Be careful," Holmes instructed. "New flames could erupt at any second."

I went into what had been the courtyard and spotted the charred remains of a man, surrounded by the smoking bodies of a number of strange creatures I doubt the most sophisticated of zoologists could identify. The human skeleton remained somewhat intact; most people don't know it takes a minimum of 800 degrees Fahrenheit to fully consume a human body. Remembering Holmes' technique of describing a man from a few measurements, I noted the length of bone, its remaining mass, the approximate size of the rib cage.

Two of the sailors ran past me, yelling, "Fire!"

Indeed, new flames had broken out in an outbuilding which had somehow been spared before. I followed the sailors as quickly as I could, my bad leg choosing this moment to seize up. Holmes, though, kept poking around the main house as if nothing new or unusual were happening.

"Holmes, for God's sake! There's another building on fire!" I yelled.

"The wind is blowing the smoke away from us," he said, completely unperturbed. "I'll be along presently, Watson."

For what seemed to me like several hours (though it

was more like ten minutes), Holmes explored the compound before returning to our party. Finally, I was able to share my data with Holmes.

"A body that size and shape certainly fits the description of Alexandre Moreau," Holmes said. "We appear to be too late. Whoever cleared this place out did a thorough job. I found nothing but the melted instruments of torture and the remains of a few cages inside the House of Pain."

"So you think the fire was set deliberately?"

"No, take a look over at that shed. They kept their food supplies in there. The flash point—"

"What's that?" I asked.

"The spot where the fire ignited," Holmes said. "The fire started when a wooden chair caught flame, which then spread to wooden barrels and, eventually, the thatched roof. I found some broken glass and metal over there, and it could have been a lamp. No deliberate arsonist would go about it that way, and it's not as if there are any authorities here to investigate and prosecute. No, clearly an unfortunate accident, but at least it has put an end to the Moreau horrors."

We prepared to leave, thinking our work done, but we heard sounds of fighting on the beach. Rushing to the scene, we saw several sailors grappling with some Moreau monsters, Challenger at the center of the melee.

On seeing us, a young woman who apparently had accompanied the other party, bolted in our direction when she saw us.

"You must help us!" she cried, in French. "They attacked from nowhere!"

I could see a hyena with severely porcine qualities, and absurdly wondered why anyone would waste good pork in such a manner. But the creature's teeth and claws had made short and bloody work of one French sailor and had trapped a second by the foot.

"Watson! Your Webley!"

"Sorry, Holmes. We were so eager to get here I left it on the ship."

Challenger, enraged, slammed his fists against the creature's snout, causing a bellow of pain and freeing the trapped French sailor. But he also caught the monster's attention, and it leapt for his throat.

"You must die!" it snarled.

"George!" the girl cried. "George!"

Our men had remembered their knives, and the blades flashed in the hot sunshine as they plunged into the hyena-swine's haunches and torso. Now wounded and bleeding, it turned and fled into the forest, leaving us to deal with the other ape-like savages.

"Leave us!" said one, some sort of combined wolf, rat, and something else. "Leave us, Men of the Sea!"

"Wait!" cried Holmes. "Where is the Creator?"

The beast pointed to the sky.

"The Man Who Walks in the Sea has told us he now watches us from the sky," it said. "Is there still Law?"

"Not here," Holmes replied. "We have no quarrel with you. Leave in peace. May fortune be with you."

The man-beast held a hand up and showed an open palm, spreading its curled and clawed fingers apart. Most of us saluted in kind, and the two abominations disappeared into the forest. Looking up, I saw something else: an orangutan climbing into one of the coconut trees, foraging.

"Let's go," said the coxswain. "I've had all I can take of this cursed island."

The French sailors regrouped, having wrapped their fallen comrade in a tarpaulin from one of their boats. The situation might have been solemn, but for a raging row between Challenger and the young woman.

"Sophie, I know you're upset and frightened,"

Challenger said, trying to be soothing, but coming across like a headmaster trying not to discipline a rambunctious pupil. "But please think of—"

"This isn't science!" she barked. "It's blasphemy! Those—those monsters have no business in nature! I will have nothing to do with it!"

"But—our plans!" Challenger pleaded.

"Go back to the boat! My plans have changed!"

Sophie Moreau (as I now know her to be) tore a wedding band from her hand, slammed it down into the sand, and marched over to Holmes and myself, followed by a pleading Challenger.

"Do you have room on your vessel for one more?" she asked. "I have money."

"I believe we can find a place," said Holmes, who seemed to be taking a mean and childish satisfaction from the stunned look on Challenger's face. "I'm leaving at our next port of call in any event. By an interesting stroke of fortune, I've been summoned to Sumatra once again. The Netherland Sumatra Company is missing a great deal of money, and there seems to be political intrigue afoot. You can still change your mind, Watson."

I shook my head.

"I have memories of my time in San Francisco, and I'd like to look up a few old friends," I said. "I have nothing on at present, and a holiday seems in order. Besides, I have been writing my reminiscences on this voyage, and this will allow me to complete the study in scarlet I have mentioned to you."

"San Francisco?" asked Sophie, her eyes bright. "In America?"

"Yes."

"I have never seen America," she said. "Please let me join you until I decide what to do."

"I'd be delighted, my dear."

"Come back with me, Sophie!" Challenger pleaded. "You can't just throw everything away over one bad incident!"

"I not only can, I feel I must," Sophie said, her voice softening. "This is far more than a bad incident. The things my uncle has wrought must never, ever leave this island. I do not understand how you could admire such a monster, George. I cannot marry someone like that. I also have the family's reputation to think of. Better we had left this alone."

"I will use his work for the good of mankind," Challenger said. "Holmes, tell her! Tell her about Moreau! This need not be for nothing."

"I'm afraid it is, Challenger," said Holmes. "Dr. Moreau is dead and the laboratory has burned to the ground. All his notes, all his research burned with it. All that remains of Dr. Moreau is a pile of smoking wood. We found his body and the remains of his pitiful experiments on a funeral pyre. Face it, Challenger. We went through all this travail for nothing."

"Have we?" Challenger tried one last time. "It's all gone, Sophie. Can't we just put the whole thing behind us?"

Sophie shook her head.

"It's too late," she said. "My work has always been devoted to beauty and betterment, George. You know that. There is no beauty in these wretches, and there never can be. I know now that I was so desperate in my situation, I convinced myself I was in love with you. I had never met a man of such energy and verve before, and I believe that's what attracted me to you. Now I believe I was just using you as a means of escape from my family and their plans for me. I'm not sure I felt love at all, just passion."

"It will never be 'just passion' for me," Challenger said. "I do love you, Sophie. No other woman has moved my heart the way you have. Please don't take my happiness away."

"Do you really think I would be happy as the wife of a professor?"

"Yes. We can work together. Please come back with me. We can make it work."

At that moment, Sophie looked up at the orangutan in the trees, and waved her hand at it in greeting. The creature looked back at her, its face impassive, but clearly fixed on Sophie Moreau. Then it raised a paw to her, as if to say goodbye before disappearing into the lush, green jungle.

"You know that ape?" I asked.

"It was to have been one of Uncle Alexandre's experiments," she said. "I felt sorry for him. It eases my heart to know he won't come to a sad, wretched end."

Challenger tried to say something, but Sophie silenced him.

"You would have let that magnificent creature suffer the torments of the damned," she said. "Just for glory."

"Were there other animals?" Holmes asked.

"Captain Vigneault freed the animals we brought here," Sophie replied. "We had no place else to take them, and certainly not enough food for a return voyage."

Poor Challenger looked on, looking for all the world like a child who's seen his puppy drown. Sophie embraced Challenger and said, "I'm sorry, George. I'll always keep you in my heart."

With that, she gave him a gentle final kiss and turned away.

For once in his life, G. E. Challenger had nothing to say. His shoulders slumped in dejection, he returned to the *Meribelle* with the other French sailors, who promised to send Sophie's belongings over to our ship.

Holmes stared at the trees, his countenance wistful.

"Come on, Holmes, don't start philosophizing now. We have a voyage to complete."

"I was just thinking, Watson, of what we might find if we return in ten years' time. Who knows if these creatures will survive? Perhaps evolve? Alexandre Moreau may have achieved greatness after all."

"He's achieved ignominy, and deservedly so. Come on, my dear Holmes."

EPILOGUE – 1896

At last, Holmes has finished reading *The Island of Doctor Moreau,* the sensational posthumous account by a chap named Edward Prendick, who claims to have spent about a year on that hellhole in the middle of the Pacific.

"I wish I had known about this man sooner," Holmes said, "but he does confirm everything I surmised from the compound's wreckage. He died never knowing how close he came to rescue."

"Do you doubt him, Holmes?"

"No, I believe he is being quite truthful, and his dating, precarious as it is, does hold up. All he'd have had to do is stay put, but that hyena thing drove him to desperation."

"One can't blame him for heading to the other side of the island," said I. "We saw for ourselves how dangerous the place was."

"Indeed."

"Since Moreau has now been exposed, perhaps I might reveal the full tale?"

"The Giant Rat of Sumatra? I'm sorry, Watson. One account from a slightly mad hermit won't get anyone's scientific curiosity going, but an account from you or me would be a vastly different affair. I do not believe it will benefit Londoners in any way to learn how close they came to being overrun by enormous, intelligent rats. I will have no hand in perpetuating the legacy of Alexandre Moreau, thank you."

"Holmes, nothing you do can stop the advance of science. Sooner or later, someone else will stumble into Moreau's footsteps. It is as inevitable as the sunrise."

"But perhaps by then ethics as well as science will have advanced. At the very least, we should wait until

148

Challenger is dead. I should hate to have someone that volatile take it into his head to get going, assuming he hasn't done so already."

"Who would let him?"

"Speaking of the Moreau family, you never did tell me your adventures in San Francisco. Were you able to work the famed Watson charm upon the young lady?"

"That's not the sort of question a gentleman answers, old fellow."

Holmes smiled and said, "No gentleman, yet I feel perfectly comfortable putting the question to you."

I smiled. Holmes likes his occasional jest.

"Well, if you must know, we spent a pleasant time together on the *Delta*, and I lost track of her not long after we docked in Sam Francisco. She decided to tour the continent, and booked passage to the East Coast. I have not heard from her since."

"I have," said Holmes, handing me a newspaper. "Check the second column."

It took a second, but I spotted the item. The Royal Horticultural Society's annual flower show is scheduled for the weekend; the prize flower this year is the Moreau Rose, the result of patient hybrid experiments by Dr. Sophie Moreau.

"Unusually educated for a woman," Holmes said. "It would be interesting to know how she came by her advanced education."

"It doesn't surprise me, Holmes. Sophie is an exceptional young woman."

"Indeed she is. Let's hope she doesn't get any ideas about animals."

With that, Holmes topped up my whiskey, picked up his violin, and filled our rooms with sweet music.

Also by Stephen Seitz

Sherlock Holmes and the Plague of Dracula

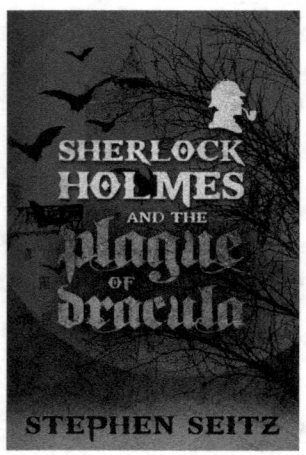

After Mina Murray asks Sherlock Holmes to locate her fiancee, Holmes and Watson travel to a land far eerier than the moors they had known when pursuing the Hound of the Baskervilles. The confrontation with Count Dracula threatens Holmes' health, his sanity, and his life. Will Holmes survive his battle with Count Dracula?

www.seitzbooks.com

Also by Stephen Seitz

Never Meant to Be

An accident with H.G. Wells' time machine strands Cynthia Kenyon in London, 1882. Utterly alone, the prisoner of Professor James Moriarty, there is but one name from the period Cynthia knows: Sherlock Holmes. What she could not know is how powerful an attraction she would feel for Holmes' partner, the handsome Dr. John Watson. Cynthia faces a number of dangerous choices on this unique journey: allow the 19th century's great criminal mastermind to plunder the centuries? Give up her family, friends, and career for the love of one man from the past? Should she correct the history she has changed, and how? No matter what Cynthia chooses, some things are never meant to be.

www.seitzbooks.com

The Ace Herron Mysteries

Secrets Can't be Kept Forever

An advertising salesman facing embezzlement charges takes his son and disappears. As Ace Herron, the crime reporter for a Vermont newspaper, pursues the case, the mystery grows deeper. Who is this man? What happened to the boy? Where did the money go? And does Ace have a rival for his wife's affections? The answers to these and other questions lead Ace on a journey to uncover dark secrets of the past, deeply hidden secrets which can't be kept forever.

Terror Strikes Downtown

A typical spring day in the town of Valentine, Vermont: golden sunshine and green hills on the outside, while embezzlement and extortion lie underneath, where desperation rules the lives of many. Deadly explosions suddenly rock the town, spreading fear and terror, leading to panic and violence, leaving dozens of dead bodies and wounded souls in their wake. Rumors of terrorism fly through town, and the lives of many are changed forever. It is up to crime reporter Ace Herron to sort the truth from the fantasy, to bring sanity to speculation, not to mention beating national media. The case could make his career, but standing in the way is Enoch Teed, a hostile editor who wants a certain kind of newsroom: one without Ace Herron in it.

www.seitzbooks.com

Also from MX Publishing

MX Publishing is the world's largest specialist Sherlock Holmes publisher, with over a hundred titles and fifty authors creating the latest in Sherlock Holmes fiction and non-fiction.

From traditional short stories and novels to travel guides and quiz books, MX Publishing cater for all Holmes fans.

The collection includes leading titles such as *Benedict Cumberbatch In Transition* and *The Norwood Author* which won the 2011 Howlett Award (Sherlock Holmes Book of the Year).

MX Publishing also has one of the largest communities of Holmes fans on Facebook with regular contributions from dozens of authors.

www.mxpublishing.com

Also from MX Publishing

Our bestselling short story collections 'Lost Stories of Sherlock Holmes', 'The Outstanding Mysteries of Sherlock Holmes', 'Untold Adventures of Sherlock Holmes' (and the sequel 'Studies in Legacy') and 'Sherlock Holmes in Pursuit'.

www.mxpublishing.com

154

Also From MX Publishing

London, 1920: Boston-bred Enoch Hale, working as a reporter for the Central Press Syndicate, arrives on the scene shortly after a music hall escape artist is found hanging from the ceiling in his dressing room. What at first appears to be a suicide turns out to be murder . . .

www.mxpublishing.com

Also from MX Publishing

Lego Sherlock Holmes

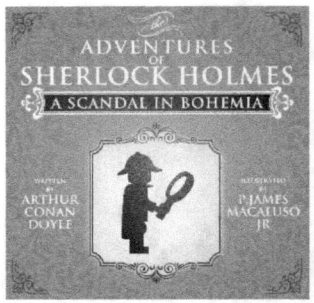 

Six original adventures from Sir Arthur Conan Doyle,
re-illustrated in Lego.

In this book series, the short stories comprising The Adventures of
Sherlock Holmes have been amusingly illustrated using only
Lego® brand minifigures and bricks. The illustrations recreate,
through custom designed Lego models, the composition of the
black and white drawings by Sidney Paget that accompanied the
original publication of these adventures appearing in The Strand
Magazine from July 1891 to June 1892.

www.mxpublishing.com

Also from MX Publishing

"Phil Growick's, 'The Secret Journal of Dr Watson', is an adventure which takes place in the latter part of Holmes and Watson's lives. They are entrusted by HM Government (although not officially) and the King no less to undertake a rescue mission to save the Romanovs, Russia's Royal family from a grisly end at the hand of the Bolsheviks. There is a wealth of detail in the story but not so much as would detract us from the enjoyment of the story. Espionage, counter-espionage, the ace of spies himself, double-agents, double-crossers...all these flit across the pages in a realistic and exciting way. All the characters are extremely well-drawn and Mr Growick, most importantly, does not falter with a very good ear for Holmesian dialogue indeed. Highly recommended. A five-star effort."

The Baker Street Society